Anabella carefully folded the letters and placed them in a box on her dressing table that held her precious items.

Thrilled as she was to hear his warm words of love and devotion, she now faced a true dilemma. Two men desired her presence at the same duel. Each wanted her to witness his triumph over the other, thus establishing his honor. One man she had come to despise for his lies and trickery. The other she loved in spite of his foolishness.

What would be the influence of her presence on either? On both? If she went with Bianca to Terni, she most certainly would have to be a witness. And Albret's mother had even recommended she support her man. Marco would not prevent her and might very well be a witness himself. If she stayed in Florence, Albret said he would come to her; thus he didn't *expect* her to be present. That certainly would be the easier course.

BARBARA YOUREE has authored six children's books as well as numerous stories and articles. She was a contributing editor of *Potpourri: A Magazine of the Literary Arts,* and a docent at the Nelson-Atkins Museum of Art in Kansas City, Missouri. She now makes her home in Arkansas.

Books by Barbara Youree

HEARTSONG PRESENTS
HP416—Both Sides of the Easel
HP483—Forever Is Not Long Enough
HP628—Silent Heart

Duel
Love

Barbara Youree

Heartsong Presents

A note from the Author:
*I love to hear from my readers! You may correspond with
me by writing:*

Barbara Youree
Author Relations
PO Box 719
Uhrichsville, OH 44683

ISBN 1-59310-791-9

DUEL LOVE

All scripture quotations are taken from the King James Version of the
Bible.

All of the characters and events in this book are fictitious. Any resem-
blance to actual persons, living or dead, or to actual events is purely
coincidental.

*Our mission is to publish and distribute inspirational products offering
exceptional value and biblical encouragement to the masses.*

PRINTED IN THE U.S.A.

one

Anabella Biliverti sat in the huge, empty ballroom of the newly constructed villa on the outskirts of Florence. Her mouth twisted in thought as she marked on her sketch sheet the corner of the room for stringed instruments. Because of her talented eye for decor, her mother and new stepfather had encouraged her to present a design for the ballroom. She relished this responsibility—rare, she knew, for a mere girl of fifteen.

Pausing from the work that delighted her, she stretched out her arms. A smile dimpled her cheeks as she closed her eyes and imagined the sketch coming to life. She saw herself in the arms of the man she so adored, swirling around the imagined room to music of forgotten origin.

She recalled another ballroom in the Biliverti family castle in Terni where she had grown up—the one locked and forgotten after the death of her father. The musty-smelling one, opened—with her mother's permission—by the castle's charming young overseer, Albret. The one where she had taught Albret to dance.

A tap on the door interrupted her reverie.

"*Signorina* Anabella?" the tentative voice of a former street urchin, now a house servant, called.

Anabella laid down her charcoal and wiped her hands on a cloth. She sighed at the interruption of her concentration but politely said, "You may come in, Giorgio. What is it?"

Giorgio, a boy of sixteen, quietly opened the door and bowed as he had been instructed. "There is a gentleman to see you, signorina, a *Signore* Albret Maseo."

She stood and blushed with excitement. "Tell him. . .tell him I will meet with him in thirty minutes in the receiving room. . .no, in the garden courtyard. I must change my dress, arrange my hair. . ." She fingered the dark curls tied behind and cascading down her back. "But don't tell him that last part."

"Signorina, please pardon me, but the gentleman said he must see you right away as he has only a few minutes. He is in the receiving room."

Giorgio bowed low and held the door open for her as she rushed past.

I look frightful, she thought. She had not seen Albret for several months—not since the peasant uprising had postponed their betrothal. He would have to accept her as she was. She tingled with anticipation and pinched her cheeks for color. *What brings him here from battle in mid-morning? Good or bad news?* None of his letters indicated he might pay her a visit. The last note had been short and impersonal, not enhanced by his usual expressions of love.

Albret stood in the middle of the room, black velvet military hat in hand and battle sword at his side. Wayward brown locks hung just below his ears and framed his handsome, clean-shaven face.

Anabella gasped with pleasure. He appeared taller than when she last saw him, maturer than his nineteen years, with broader shoulders and a more muscular frame. "I wasn't expecting you," she stammered as she removed her charcoal-smudged apron. She handed it to a girl slightly older than herself who had followed her in as a chaperone.

"That will be all, Luisa. You may go. The gentleman is my betrothed—or soon will be—so we may be left alone." She smiled at Albret, and Luisa bowed and backed out of the room.

Albret touched her cheek gently. A corner of his mouth curled upward, stopping short of a smile. "I see you've been playing with charcoal again," he said, rubbing the smudge off with his thumb.

He took both of Anabella's hands. More seriously, he looked intensely into her eyes and said, "I must talk to you. My captain has sent me to approach a sympathetic Florentine merchant about supplies, and I have made a quick detour to come here. I wish I could explain all that is in my heart, but I must return tonight. We are camped this side of Siena—the closest I have been to you."

"I wish you could stay—I miss you so." She longed to feel his lips on hers, but his mind seemed far from romance. She searched his face for clues to his intent but could discern nothing.

"Anabella, I love you as always. Do you believe that?"

"Yes, of course. I love you and await only for this uprising to be put down so we can finalize our betrothal," she said cheerfully. "Let us sit down. I will call for refreshments and listen to what you have to say." She stepped toward the settee, but he gripped her hand and stood firm.

"Anabella, I am *with* the uprising. That is the problem. You are nobility. I am not. As a servant, I've lived most of my life in grand houses, though they were not *my* houses—neither by blood nor by achievement. When your brother, Marco, offered me your hand in marriage, I was both startled and delighted. Though I loved you deeply, marriage was but a distant fantasy because of our difference in status. I convinced myself it was of little importance. Now, as I fight this struggle with the peasants, I've come to realize it is truly a great gulf between us."

She stood facing him, her hands still in his. His palms felt warm and calloused—hers cool and moist with perspiration as if blood were draining from them. Without taking her eyes from his, she became aware of the newly furnished receiving room—the gold-embroidered, satin draperies; the elaborately carved chairs and table; the hand-painted oil lamp. She was proud of these furnishings and had selected the lamp herself. But they were only things. Was Albret placing greater importance on such possessions above their love?

Albret squeezed her hands but averted his eyes. "The peasants have a just cause. When I left with the men of Terni to join those of Siena, I did not know the full story of their grievance. I've now learned that a nobleman whose great-grandfather gave each peasant family a small parcel of land near Siena to build their huts and plant their vegetables has not honored the agreement. This was a verbal contract. He had said they and their descendants could live there as long as they farmed his plantation."

"That seems like a fair arrangement," said Anabella. She frowned, trying to make sense of what he was telling her.

"But now the present *conte* wants them off the land so he can raise sheep. Wool brings a greater profit today and takes fewer workers. They went to him to negotiate, but he set his thugs against them. This started the conflict."

"I thought they were fighting over excessive burdens and unjust taxes imposed by King Philip of Spain, to whom we all must answer."

"Yes, that is part of the rebellion." He released her hands and paced about the room. "And yes, all Tuscany is under the Spanish king, but the nobility pay no taxes—none at all." He pulled a handkerchief from his sleeve and wiped perspiration from his brow. "Other peasants joined the cause because of their own grievances as well as sympathy over the land issue. That is why some of our workers from your brother's *seigniory* in Terni left to join—"

"I know, Albret. And you agreed to lead their squadron." She stood awkwardly alone and watched him pace.

"Don't you see, Anabella? I am fighting the cause of the poor against the nobility. *You* are nobility." He stood facing her now and seemed to plead for her understanding.

"So you hold that against me?" She took a step back from him. *Is he thinking of me as part of the enemy?* "I didn't make the laws. Nor did I choose what family to be born into—"

"No, no, Anabella. I hold no blame against you or your

family. I know how you care for orphan children here in Florence. Your brother, the marchese, released me to fight with the peasants. This unjust conte is related to the owner of lands in Terni right next to your brother's seigniory. As a neighbor, Marco could have supported him. However, as I fight with the peasants for their concerns, I've become starkly aware of the differences."

"But Marco elevated you to overseer of our seigniory. He himself proposed our betrothal and in addition to my dowry will give us land and build us a villa."

Albret placed his hands on her shoulders and looked into her upturned face. "But Anabella, *I* am not nobility. I appreciate your brother's generosity, I do. But what do I have to offer you? I have no noble inheritance of my own. I have not built up wealth as a merchant or banker. Until two years ago, I worked for the marchese—rather the marchese's wife—as a house servant. My mother is still serving her. I have no deeds of valor—"

"Albret, what are you saying?" Her questioning eyes searched his.

"I am saying I do not feel right about our betrothal, not until I have *earned* the right to be your husband—someone of whom you can be proud. As a matter of deepest honor, I believe it is only right to tell you this and release you to seek another. That is what I have come to say."

Anabella's mouth fell open in shock. The room suddenly felt stuffy. She could smell the newness of the fabric in the drapes and chairs condemning her. The two stood facing each other, no longer touching. He was still there. Perhaps he was having second thoughts. *Doesn't he realize how he is hurting me? Doesn't he know the strength of our love?* Anger engulfed her. She felt its heat surge through her body and burn her cheeks. *He is rejecting me!*

"Please understand, Anabella," he said softly. "I am frustrated, perhaps confused. But I thought you should know my feelings. When this insurgency is settled, we will talk again. In all honor, I cannot ask you to wait for me."

"Then good-bye, Albret, and may God protect you in battle." The words sounded hollow in her own ears. Their eyes met briefly. Her mouth felt dry and her body numb. As no other words came to her, she swirled her skirts around and walked briskly out of the room.

She heard Albret's strained voice behind her. "Good-bye, Anabella. May God bless you always."

Anabella snatched her apron from Luisa, who had stood guard outside the room, and ran up the wide, sweeping staircase to a landing halfway up. Hot tears stung her eyes, and she muffled her sobs with her handkerchief. From a narrow window, she watched as Albret took the reins of his horse from a groom, mounted, galloped from the villa to the main road, and disappeared behind a grove of elm trees. Anger melted, but confusion took over. She yearned for his arms about her, drawing her close, effacing the emptiness.

two

Albret rode at full speed toward the merchant's house in Florence to attend to his errand. He knew Signore Paolo personally because Anabella's stepfather, Antonio Turati, was in the process of selling the active part of his merchandising business to him. Albret had offered to approach him for support of their cause.

Not until he'd accomplished this did he allow his mind to dwell on the other honorable mission—that of rescinding his betrothal to the lovely Anabella, whom he loved with all his heart. He recalled her large, innocent eyes looking up at him, expecting love; her softly rounded body desiring his arms about her; her words: "I wish you could stay—I miss you so." But surely he had done the right thing, the honorable thing, to free her until he could present himself as a man worthy of her love.

He arrived back at camp around midnight and gave the password to the sentry on duty, tied his horse, and headed directly toward his captain's tent. The light of a whale-oil lamp glowed from within, casting a man's shadow on the canvas. He whispered, "Captain Gaza?"

"Come in, Albret," said the captain.

The young man lifted the flap and found the captain sitting cross-legged, studying a hand-drawn map of the region. "What did you gain from our sympathetic merchant?"

Albret squatted, removed his cap, and ran his fingers through his hair. "Indeed, he is in sympathy with our cause as I suspected. He will send two wagonloads of supplies—food, clothing, guns, and gunpowder."

"Good, but didn't you tell him we use daggers?"

"He laughed when I told him that," said Albret. "He said daggers are useless against gentlemen's swords. Besides, the thugs the conte has hired—though no better than our peasants at one-on-one combat—are skilled in banditry and treachery."

"I see. Go on."

"The peasants—except those from Terni—know the Siena countryside better than the conte's mercenaries. Ambush must be our strategy. He said we must strike with guns from cover, not daggers in the open."

"Good," said Captain Gaza. "When will the supplies and guns arrive?"

"Day following the morrow. I explained how the peasants first attempted negotiation. I told how the conte rejected any compromise and struck first with a cannon blast on your house, Captain, killing your young son. When I said that, the merchant shook his head and promised more help in the future. But he made me promise to keep his identity a secret. He is well known around Florence and Siena. To protect his new business, he doesn't want word to leak."

"It won't. I don't even know his name." The flame in the lamp flickered and burned low.

"We'll need to train the men to use guns and powder," said Albret, aware that guns in the hands of untrained men would be dangerous.

"Not much time for that. We have perhaps a dozen fellows who can instruct the others. Many will prefer the weapons they are used to." The captain folded his map and shook the young man's hand. "Good work, Albret. Now get some rest."

The flame sputtered once and went out as Albret left the tent.

Most of the men slept in the open without shelter of tents. He stumbled in the dark over a few soldiers who cursed him in their sleep, and slipped back the way he had come to the guard's post outside the camp.

"Ho, Massetti," he whispered.

"Yeah, I'm awake. That you, Albret?"

"Indeed, it is I."

"So did you find the merchant that might help us?" whispered Massetti.

"I did. He's sending supplies, including guns." Albret sat down facing the guard and leaned against a tree.

"I've shot a gun before. It's a good weapon. And did you see your lady?"

"Yes." Albret remained silent several minutes, then said, "I don't think she took my words well. But I cannot fight against the privileged nobility and then marry into a noble family and accept, unearned, all their privileges. That would not be honorable. Marco wants to build us a grand villa and grant us a portion of his land in Terni as well as bestow her dowry."

"You are so young, Albret. At nineteen, how can you know what is best? I have a wife and three children, one boy already apprenticed to a shoemaker. All my decisions are based on what is best for them. If this rebellion had broken out during grape harvest, I would not be here. But now we have finished that work, and the marchese does not need me for a while, so I can fight for this just cause. Have you thought of what is best for Anabella? Would she be happier in someone else's grand villa or in a small cottage you could build for her?"

"I don't rightly know. I first met her in Rome while I was serving Bianca, who later married her brother, Marco, now the marchese. Anabella's father had just died, and their half brother had confiscated the castle, sending them and their mother into exile in Rome. Anabella was just ten or eleven years old then. They lived in a small townhouse with only one servant until the marchese was able to reclaim what was rightfully theirs."

"Yes, I know," Massetti said, shaking his head. "The marchese hired me to work in the fields shortly after his return."

"Anabella was not unhappy in those circumstances. She and her mother sold needlework in the marketplace while her brother worked as a stonemason. They weren't destitute like so many deposed nobles. But I do remember her concern, young as she was, that her brother would never be able to find a nobleman for her to marry. I think she would be happier in a villa, to answer your question."

Albret broke a dry stick in two and threw the pieces down hard. "She loves decorating, selecting fabrics, designing rooms. . . It will just have to be another man's villa."

"Won't she wait for you? You know, until you make something of yourself on your own. You are both so young."

"I released her. I told her she was free to see another."

A twig snapped. The sentry drew his dagger and Albret reached for his sword, which lay beside him on the ground. They waited in silence, scarcely breathing.

A small furry animal scurried and disappeared into the brush. Massetti put away his dagger and continued their conversation. "But will she seek to see others? She loves you, does she not?"

"Maybe not now. I believe she was angry, but she may well thank me later."

"Get some sleep, my friend. We should be safe tonight. Scouts have reported no trace of the enemy in the vicinity, and sentries are posted all around. But most likely, we'll have battles to fight tomorrow." Massetti's relief sentry came up at that moment.

Albret lay on his back in the dry grass with his head on his velvet cap. Through the treetops he could make out one faint star. As he stared at it, he felt Anabella was equally far from him. Silently, he prayed to God for her protection and for guidance and courage in battle. Then, weary from travel and emotion, he drifted off to sleep.

❧

The squadron awoke to a cannon blast, violently splintering the trees—and leaving five dead peasants and a dozen or more wounded. Gunfire and an onslaught of sword-wielding warriors followed. Albret sprang to his feet just as the captain shouted, "To arms!" He brushed debris from his clothing, mounted his horse, drew his sword, and charged toward the attackers.

In spite of the scouts' report, somehow the conte's men had pulled a cannon through the woods and laid in wait till dawn to make the surprise attack. Albret fought with advantage until he was toppled from his horse early in combat. When his steed fled, he was forced to fight on foot alongside the brave peasants, all with empty stomachs.

Outnumbered, outgunned, and inferior in swordsmanship, they were beaten to a retreat. As they carried their wounded back through the woods, Albret spied the conte himself sitting astride a horse in an open area and laughing uproariously.

At the sight of the jeering conte, Albret's blood simmered with anger. He strode into the open space and shouted, "You coward! Why don't you fight on equal footing with your adversaries?"

"Indeed, I shall," retorted the conte with seething sarcasm. "I'll come down to your level—which still leaves me the superior." He leaped from his horse and ran toward Albret, sword drawn. "You puny peasant! You don't deserve death by a gentleman's sword. *En garde!*"

Their swords clashed. At first Albret held the advantage. He parried, turned, and thrust—and brought the first blood as his blade grazed the back of the conte's right wrist. But weakened from battle, he found himself no match for the rested conte, who had apparently remained behind his troops. In no time, the conte forced Albret on his back, pinning him to the ground by spearing his sword through an upper arm muscle. The conte pressed his knee on Albret's chest and glared into his eyes.

"Don't dare to call this conte a coward, you swine," he snarled. Then pausing, he wrinkled his brow, looked into Albret's eyes, and said, "I know that face. I've seen it somewhere before." With a violent yank, he pulled his sword from Albret's left arm. "You're no peasant after all—a bigger prize, I think. One that requires an audience for your demise!

I'll save you for another day, you scum. We'll fight a duel of honor. Then we'll see who's the coward!"

The conte roared with laughter as he mounted his horse. Two aides rode up just in time to escort him back to his base.

Albret writhed in agony. He tore a strip of cloth from the bottom of his shirt and attempted to tie it above the wound with his right hand and his teeth, groaning with every effort. *At least Conte Bargerino doesn't remember where he has seen me— at his uncle's carnival ball in Terni. That's where. He was dancing with Anabella. . .while I stood in the shadows, not knowing how to dance. . .or what social etiquette required.*

❧

When Albret awoke, an elderly woman stood over him wrapping his wounds. He lay on a cot in a humble hut. A chicken walked through the open door clucking contentedly, and thin curtains flapped out the windows.

"Where. . .where am I?"

"You're here in my abode, you are. But if that's to mean you're safe, I'm not so sure," the woman said, continuing her work.

Albret winced in pain. "How bad is it?"

"It's a deep gash all right. Lots of blood drained out." She finished her dressing and left the room. In a few minutes, she returned carrying a mug of cabbage soup. "Here, try this. It'll give you some strength."

"What do you mean, I might not be safe here?"

"Well, your friend rode off saying he would get the marchese to send a carriage. No carriage has ever been to this door."

"Oh, so you think I'm fighting for Conte Bargerino?" He tried to raise himself on his good elbow but fell back. "No, I'm with Captain Gaza in the squadron from Terni. The conte himself did this to me."

"That's good." She smiled and spooned some soup into his mouth. "It's not good the conte stabbed you, but it's very good you fight against him. He's a scoundrel, he is."

"So who brought me here—what friend?"

"Said his name was Massetti, and he had a scar, like from a burn, on the side of his face."

"Ah, yes," said Albret, relaxing at the name of his friend. "We both work for the marchese. He's scarred from putting out a huge fire."

"He said to tell you he found your horse. He brought you here on it, then rode off to see the marchese fellow. Sounds like an enemy to me."

"No, this marchese is neutral and a good man." He took the cup with his right hand and drank from it in gulps. "What do you know about Conte Bargerino, my dear woman?"

She refilled the cup and tore off a chunk of stale bread for him. After pulling a chair up beside his bed, she eagerly told what she knew. "The rumor has it—and these rumors are apt to be true as daylight—that Conte Bargerino came among us pretending to be a peasant, the likes of us. He wore tattered clothes and a rag about his head. His hair and beard were rightly unkempt, but it's hard to hide the soft hands of the rich."

Albret finished his meal and lay back refreshed but still weak. "Why would he want to disguise himself?"

"He already knew we were upset that he was ordering us all off our land so he could raise sheep next spring. We have no place to go. Our families have worked for his family for generations. His father was a hard taskmaster, but he paid us and gave us no mind. Then when the old conte died a year back, this heir took over, bringing troubles of every sort with him."

"So why the disguise?" Albret wanted to get as much information as possible, but with the intense pain, he found it difficult to concentrate.

The woman sucked in her lips over sparse teeth, apparently determined to leave no detail unshared. "You see, he was going about among us, trying to stir up resentment toward the Spaniards and saying that if we revolted we could get relief of our taxes and maybe not have to work on the roads a whole month out of every year with no pay at all. We thought this wise fellow—for no one guessed who he really was—would lead us to do just that. But all of a sudden, he disappeared. Since everyone was all stirred up against the king, the men decided to do just what he'd suggested."

"But that doesn't make sense. Why would the conte stir up a rebellion against himself?"

"Well, like I said, he knew we were already angry at him. This is where the rumor comes in. Before taking up arms, the villagers chose a group of men to go negotiate with Conte Bargerino, not knowing, of course, at that time he was actually the same fellow that had been posing as a peasant. They had all decided among themselves what to demand of their overlord.

"More than half the families were willing to accept just compensation for the land, because after all, it had been promised to their forebears as long as their descendants worked it. Any fair person could see that ordering people out of their homes and off the land they claimed in good faith was unjust and not worthy of a nobleman. They just wanted enough money in exchange to move into Florence and get jobs in the factories. The rest asked to stay on the land and be hired to work with his sheep."

The old woman's eyes sparkled with excitement. "See, one of the conte's servants, whose family lives here among us, tipped the men off after they left his castle. This servant said outright that Conte Bargerino disguised himself as a peasant leader. He stirred us all up because he wants to impress King Philip by putting down a rebellion among the king's Italian subjects. And that way he hopes to be chosen as one of the king's grandees—whatever that is—and move to the court in Madrid and live in high style."

She slapped both hands on her knees as if to emphasize this inside knowledge. Then in a lower tone, she whispered, "Just between the two of us, I don't think the conte cares anything about raising sheep."

Albret nodded thoughtfully. "No doubt. So he came to incite a rebellion so he could gain favor with King Philip by putting it down—for his own benefit."

"Not everybody knows about his reasons," said the woman as she lowered her voice. "But we all know he fired the first cannon shot, destroying a house and killing an innocent child. We have plenty of reasons to fight against him. He's a scoundrel all right."

three

"I don't understand the thinking of men," Anabella stated flatly. She had just told her mother Albret's devastating words. They sat on a bench in the formal garden, surrounded by lingering blooms of early autumn and the sound of falling water from a three-tiered fountain.

Her mother, Costanza Turati, put her arm around her daughter's shoulders. "No woman does, my daughter. It's honor above all else. We can't blame them for that, but it's the women who suffer."

"He said something about having to build up his own wealth. He seemed almost angry when I reminded him that Marco would give us land and build us a villa." Anabella dabbed her eyes and tucked her handkerchief into her sleeve. "We love each other. Isn't that enough?"

"To our way of thinking, of course," said her mother with a smile and sigh. "Men crave admiration from a woman as much as love, I believe."

"But surely he knows I admire him. I admire his scholarship. He reads Marco's books every spare moment and has taught himself Latin." She rearranged her full skirts and gazed out over the city of Florence in the hazy distance. "He has the talent of leadership and performs admirably well as overseer of the seigniory—Marco said as much."

"But Marco took back many of those duties when he returned to take up residence again. If Albret feels he must prove himself worthy of your love, perhaps you need to be patient and wait for him to do just that." She patted her daughter's knee.

"He thinks breaking our betrothal is *honorable*. I don't

understand that at all. Two years ago, he seemed most pleased when Marco offered to arrange it. He signed the *impalmare* agreement, even though he had nothing to offer then either."

"But he was only a boy of seventeen. He's still quite young."

"He admitted he was confused. Indeed he is!" Anabella stood up and swirled her skirts about. "Well, it's his confusion, not mine!" She offered her hand to her mother, still seated on the garden bench, and noted how much she resembled her—medium height, large eyes, and full figure. Her mother's hair was tinged with gray at the temples and wound in a bun, whereas Anabella tied back her dark ringlets with a ribbon. *But, unlike me, Mother is practical and patient. She is right, of course. However, just waiting without doing something is so very hard.*

Her mother stood up, and together they walked arm in arm down the pebbled path toward the villa, past the water fountain and statuary.

"Our friends, the Soderinis, have been invited to dinner a week hence," remarked her mother in a cheerful tone. "Perhaps you would like to help Clarice plan the courses to serve—and pick and arrange some flowers for the hall vases."

"I would, indeed." She squeezed her mother's hand and smiled. "I haven't seen the Soderini sisters in some time. And thank you, Mother, for your good counsel."

&

A week later, their guests arrived. Anabella felt proud of the extravagant dinner, which she had in part planned and prepared. After the meal, her stepfather, Papa Antonio Turati, and the Signore Soderini retired to a corner of the salon to discuss business and the politics of the day, subjects they seldom spoke about to their wives and certainly not with their daughters. Anabella's mother and the Signora Soderini took places on the opposite side of the room to talk about their interests.

Anabella and the two Soderini sisters lit a whale-oil lamp in an alcove off the dining area where they could giggle and converse without disturbing their elders. The talk soon turned to the young men in their lives.

"My barone is the most genteel of men," said Cecilia Soderini. "He keeps me constantly entertained with his wry witticisms. He writes me romantic sonnets and has them delivered every Sunday afternoon by a coachman."

"Really? How extraordinary!" exclaimed Anabella, much impressed.

"Not so unusual. Many of the young noblemen we know are thus gifted, wouldn't you say, Simonetta?"

"True, yet my *visconte* is more knowledgeable about the artists," said her sister with a smile.

The three young women sat in baroque-style, brocaded chairs around a small table that held their cups of after-dinner herbal tea. Anabella had always perceived the Soderini ladies as refined, attractive, and sophisticated in their manners. She was interested in how enamored they were with the two gentlemen about whom they spoke.

Though of noble blood herself, Anabella's life until the past two years had been one of near isolation in Terni, where her family was only one of three aristocratic families. She realized, listening to these two young women, how sparse her social contacts had been.

Cecilia set down her cup and folded her hands. "I believe my father will soon arrange my betrothal to the barone."

"And that pleases you, Cecilia?" asked Anabella.

"Most certainly. The only problem is that the barone's family wants to squeeze from us a huge dowry." She raised the cup again to her lips and peered out over it. "Of course, our father can afford any amount he chooses."

"It's already more than you are worth," said her sister with a touch of sarcasm.

"Not really. Papa will consent, I am sure. Where else will they find such a worthy nobleman for me? So many nobles have been deposed of late and are forced to work at menial occupations not worthy of their station. Ah, but not Romolo, so handsome and well dressed. He just purchased a beaver hat with exotic turkey feathers from the Americas." She framed an imaginary hat with her hands above her head and drew feathers in the air.

"You should see him in it, Anabella," she continued. "He curls his mustache at the ends and wears his beard pointed in the latest fashion. How very striking he is! With my chaperone, he took me for a ride along the Arno River just yesterday. The strollers stopped to stare at his elegant carriage and horses. He thrilled them with a tip of his beaver hat."

"Well," interrupted Simonetta, "my visconte owns vast lands with sheep herds in his own name. And his family's palace is adorned with works by the famous painters Raphael, Caravaggio, and Botticelli, as well as the sculptor Donatello. He knows all about them and their artistic styles." She leaned back as if waiting for applause.

Not to be outdone, Anabella countered, "My Albret knows about art, too, and he reads sonnets in Latin."

"But does he write love sonnets to you?" asked Cecilia, fluttering a fan in front of her face.

"And does he own lands?" remarked Simonetta.

"He will when we are married," said Anabella, having not relinquished her dream of marriage to him. "My brother promised us land and a villa in the impalmare agreement." She refilled the three teacups from the kettle, then lifted her cup to her lips.

"That is good," agreed the sisters.

"At least you won't live the life of a common farmer's wife," said Simonetta. "Have you the date for your betrothal?"

Anabella felt blood drain from her face.

"I hope it is not ahead of mine," interjected Cecilia. "I'm the oldest of the three of us. I should be betrothed first."

"Perhaps you will be," said Anabella solemnly. She took a deep breath and decided to confess her situation to her closest friends. "Because Albret is not of noble blood—"

"Yes, we know. Oh, my dear Anabella!" Cecilia clasped her hands over Anabella's in a gesture of sympathy.

"Let me finish," Anabella said, withdrawing her hands. "He feels that he is not worthy of my love until he proves himself."

"You poor dear," said Simonetta. "So he broke your agreement to betroth?"

"He isn't worthy of you, dear friend. I always thought that, though I dared not say so to you. He grew up as your sister-in-law's servant. Certainly, he is well educated and intelligent enough, but. . .you seemed so enamored with the boy," said Cecilia.

"He's not a *boy*, Cecilia! And I still love him, though he released me to see others." Anabella had hoped for more comfort from her friends, but already she regretted sharing her deepest concern with them.

"You're coming to the ball three weeks hence, are you not?" said Simonetta, suddenly enthusiastic. "My visconte's family, the Strozzis, are hosting it at their palace. I'm sure your family will have an invitation."

"Probably so," said Anabella with little enthusiasm of her own.

"We will introduce you to a *conte* we know," said Cecilia. "He is handsome, very wealthy, and charming.

"Of course he is engaged in—" Simonetta clasped a hand over her mouth.

"In other affairs at the moment," her sister said hastily. "But he never misses a grand ball. Wear your finest, and we assure you that he—or someone else—can take your mind off that little Albret."

❧

A few days later after the noontime meal, Anabella lingered at the table while her parents sipped coffee. The five orphan boys they were mentoring had been dismissed for a few minutes of free time before their lessons.

"Have you finished the plans for the ballroom, Anabella?" her stepfather, Antonio, asked, pushing back his empty cup.

"Yes, Papa Antonio."

"Bring your sketches, Anabella," said her mother. "We are eager to begin furnishing it."

"They are almost complete," said the girl, delighted to show her work. "They are in the ballroom." She hurried off to retrieve them.

When she returned moments later, she stopped in the doorway, realizing she was the subject of her parents' conversation. Their backs were to the door, and their voices audible.

"At last she is again showing some interest in her project," she heard her mother say with a sigh. "She is really quite brokenhearted over Albret."

"Yet I can understand how Albret feels, Costanza," said Papa Antonio as he leaned back in his chair. "I came from more abject poverty than his and would never have asked your hand in marriage had I not risen to my present status."

"True, and I might not have paid you any mind at all," Anabella's mother said chuckling. She finished the last sip of her coffee and set aside the cup and saucer.

"I even purchased my title of barone. I am not so proud of that."

"But even if. . ."

Anabella stepped back, then reentered speaking loudly. "Here they are, Papa Antonio." *I didn't know Papa Antonio had bought his noble title. He rarely uses it.* Tucking away that interesting bit of knowledge, she spread out the sketch sheet on the table, and her parents surveyed it.

"My drawings are not so representative; that's why I have labeled everything. Here is the area for stringed instruments. And here, three chaise lounges, perhaps a dozen settees, and assorted chairs—all carved in the baroque style with brocaded satin upholstery. The color scheme I am suggesting is blue—various shades—and light tan. Blue velvet draperies—styled thus, if you can discern my meaning."

"This is all very elegant, Anabella," said her mother, inspecting the details of the design.

"Do you suppose we could commission Guido Reni to paint frescos on the vaulted ceiling?" Anabella continued. "You know, as he does on the garden houses in Rome. And perhaps El Greco could do a painting of the city of Florence like he recently finished of Toledo. I've not seen it, but Bianca says it is fabulous. However, I don't want an ominous storm in ours. Something bright and more cheerful."

"You certainly have expensive tastes," Papa Antonio said laughing. "Speaking of your sister-in-law—why don't you have Bianca paint something?"

"Of course. I—rather Mother and I—have already discussed that with Bianca. She wants to wait awhile until her baby is older."

"She plans to do the painting here while Anabella and I take care of little Pietro. Won't that be entertaining!"

"Yes, and less expensive, too, I would guess," said Papa Antonio.

"She was quite an important artist in Rome before marrying Marco. We will pay her what she is worth," said Anabella's mother with a cajoling smile.

"And what are these?" asked Papa Antonio. He stood over the sketch and pointed to two large squares with designs.

"These are just some ideas for tapestries. They would hang here and here." She leaned over the sketch and pointed.

"I know a wonderful factory in Vienna that does exquisite work," suggested Papa Antonio.

"And very expensive, I would guess," Anabella said, mocking her stepfather's concern over expense. "Could Mother and I go with you and your merchandising train and meet with the artisans? I could take my sketches."

"Perhaps, but shortly I'll be a silent partner, now that Paolo is taking over the business," said Papa Antonio. "We could go by coach, however. Perhaps this spring."

"You will spoil the child, Antonio," said her mother, teasing.

"Honestly, Anabella, you have made very artful plans," said Papa Antonio. He rolled up the design and tied a string around it. "I will look over them and calculate the cost."

"We admire your talent, my daughter, and we are both proud of you." She smiled and patted her shoulder.

Anabella shyly lowered her eyes and bowed slightly. "Thank you, Mother and Papa Antonio." She felt exhilarated by the compliments. As she walked toward the orphans' schoolroom, she thought, *This must be the feeling Albret craves from me— admiration for something he has achieved. But of course, on a much grander scale—more like Papa Antonio's business success.*

Anabella walked into the servants' dining room where five boys between the ages of seven and sixteen sat at a table, prepared for their lessons. An inkstand stood on the table, and paper and quills lay at each boy's place.

Gian, the youngest and newest addition, sat stiffly with his hands clasped tightly in his lap. He was thin and pale, not having yet benefited from good nourishment. It had been Papa Antonio's idea to rescue orphan children from the streets, then nourish and train them—just as a benefactor had once done for him. Anabella enjoyed the project as much as her parents did.

"Buona sera, signorina," the older four boys said in unison when Anabella walked in.

"Good afternoon, boys. Are we ready to begin our lesson?" With broad grins, they all nodded, and she continued. "Good. Then let's begin by writing your name at the top of your paper."

They nearly spilled the ink in their eagerness to dip their quills. Gian sat motionless. "I don't know letters," he said softly.

"Of course you don't—not yet. I'll teach you." She pulled a chair next to his, sat down, and took his quill.

Anabella's mother arrived with a large Bible.

"Buona sera, signora," all five said.

"Good afternoon, boys," said Anabella's mother. "Do you know what this is?"

"A big book?"

"It's the Holy Bible," said Giorgio, the oldest, grinning with pride. Healthy and fine featured, he already worked as a servant at the villa.

"You are correct. And we are going to read from it today."

"*We*, signora?"

"Yes, you. Each of you," she said to the older ones. Anabella's mother laid the Bible on the table and stood behind them while Anabella continued her work with the new student.

Anabella's mother read out loud, pointing to each word, "In the beginning God created the heavens and the earth." Then she asked each boy to do the same, helping them along. She showed them how to copy the words *God*, *heaven*, and *earth*.

After forty-five minutes of work, Anabella's mother announced, "Signore Turati will be here shortly. He is going to begin your lessons in horsemanship today. Have any of you ever ridden a horse?" They beamed with excitement but shook their heads.

At that moment, Papa Antonio entered and received the usual greeting. Gian solemnly held his paper up in front of him. The letters *G–I–A–N* were written in large scraggly lines, slanting downward.

"I believe that spells *Gian*," Papa Antonio said. "What a scholar you will be!"

As the women turned to leave, Papa Antonio handed Anabella a folded and sealed parchment. "This is for you—from Marco."

"Why just to me? He always addresses his letters to you and Mother."

Papa Antonio shrugged his shoulders in equal puzzlement.

Hoping it contained some word about Albret, Anabella rushed off to her room to read her message in private.

four

Albret arrived at the Biliverti castle in Terni late in the afternoon. Massetti had fetched him in the marchese's carriage, but the three-day journey, jostling over rocky roads, had left him exhausted. Albret's mother, a household servant, and the marchesa, Bianca Biliverti, met him at the front entrance. With distress written on her face, his mother offered her hand to assist him.

"No, Mother, I can manage," he said with a wan smile as he alighted. He encircled his good arm about her shoulders and kissed her on the cheek. "It's a minor wound."

"But, Son, you are feverish!" She drew back and looked at his bandages. "Your arm needs redressing. It has bled through."

"We will take good care of him, Sylvia," said the young marchesa. "And, Massetti, thank you for bringing Albret home."

"My duty, signora." Massetti bowed slightly. He then handed Albret his sword and left to tend to the horses and clean the carriage from its journey.

Albret was able to walk inside unassisted but slumped immediately into an armchair in the salon. Bianca hurriedly gathered multiple cushions and plumped them around him. His mother rushed to the pantry to fetch supplies. Together the women removed the soiled bandages as Albret winced but made no sound. His mother applied an herbal poultice to his swollen wound while the marchesa laid cold cloths on his fevered brow.

"When Massetti came for the carriage, he told us how he found you passed out and losing blood," said his mother.

"The cut will heal quickly, Mother. I just need a few days

rest before my return," he said in the strongest voice he could muster.

Albret saw the startled look in his mother's eyes. She wouldn't beg him to stay longer, but he knew she wished it.

"A servant is preparing you food and drink in the kitchen," said the marchesa. "But take repose for now."

His mother wrapped strips of cloth around the cleaned wound. She then kissed the top of his head and returned to her domestic duties.

The marchesa sat in a chair near the young soldier. "May I ask, dear Albret, if you've availed yourself of an opportunity to visit Anabella in Florence?" she said with a twinkle in her eyes. "The battle was not so far from the outskirts of the city, I understand."

Albret laid his head back into a soft pillow and closed his eyes. Bianca was like a sister to him—only two years his elder. They had grown up together as children when his mother served her parents in Rome. Her father had provided tutors for the two of them. He had served as her bodyguard from the age of fourteen, carrying a dagger for her protection. Yet he felt reluctant to speak to her of Anabella.

Finally, he said, "Yes. We visited briefly. I was on a military errand in the city."

Bianca raised her eyebrows in expectation of some details. But at that moment, a servant announced Albret's food awaited him in the kitchen—thus rescuing him from further discourse.

"Marco will be here day following the morrow," she called after him as he walked stiffly toward the kitchen.

≈

Albret spent that night and the next day in a feverish delirium. In the upstairs room the marchesa had provided for him, he tossed about in bed, suffering alternately from chilling sweats and burning fever. The marchesa, his mother, and another servant took turns tending him. He automatically thanked them all, not knowing which woman gave him sips of water or changed his bandages.

Visions of Conte Bargerino raced through his troubled dreams. The conte towered over him, much larger than life, and inflicted the stab wound time and again. He would awaken to the throbbing pain in his swollen arm. He wondered how his fellow insurgents were faring in battle. Only briefly did the conte's threat of a duel of honor cross his muddled mind.

On the morning of the third day, his fever broke. Rays of sunlight pierced through the east windows of the room. He squinted his eyes and wondered for a few moments where he might be and why. Recalling the essentials, he arose, bathed, and dressed in the clean clothes set out for him. He would shave later.

Weak from his ordeal, he descended the staircase. As the castle seemed eerily devoid of all inhabitants save himself, he wandered to the kitchen and prepared a pot of herbal tea. *Ah, this must be Sunday, thus the servants' day off and the day of worship for them as well as the Bilivertis,* he thought as he nibbled on stale bread and cheese. *I must return to the battlefront.*

Instinctively, he sought the little alcove between the servants' quarters and the kitchen. Here he had spent his leisure hours when he and his mother had come to live in the castle after Bianca's marriage to Anabella's brother. Most of the servants and vineyard workers lived in town or in outbuildings on the estate, but he and his mother were granted special privileges. She roomed next to the new marchesa as her personal attendant. He had been given indoor quarters adjacent to that of the head chef.

In those days, the marchese Marco Biliverti and his wife, Bianca, lived away at the University of Padua where the marchese was pursuing his studies under the famous astronomer and physicist Galileo. The widow, Signora Costanza Biliverti, the marchese's mother, held authority in his absence, and her daughter, the lovely Anabella, tugged at the reins of Albret's heart.

This morning he sat on the familiar window seat in the alcove and thumbed through the few scientific books left there by the marchese for him to read as he chose. He picked up a handwritten manuscript by the great Galileo himself, titled *The Medicean Stars*. As he read, he learned the text concerned the astronomer's discovery of four bright satellites circling Jupiter. He had named them for the Medici family that ruled his home region of Tuscany.

Intrigued as Albret was by this new knowledge, his mind wandered to his first private conversation with Anabella. She had just ended a period of mourning after the death of an elderly servant. He remembered her face was fresh and radiant and her lips full and pink. He had been reading a poem by Virgil on this very window seat when she came up to him.

Their talk had centered on the servant whom they both suspected had been murdered—and later learned that indeed he had. Then her conversation had turned—with much excitement on her part—to her impending betrothal. A man who claimed to be a nobleman had come that morning seeking her brother's consent. Albret also recalled how unworthy he had felt, sitting in the alcove with the girl he loved with all his heart as she enthused about the handsome nobleman. Later they all learned that this man's family was not noble at all and had been behind the murder of the servant.

As his friendship with Anabella had developed, Albret had tried to extinguish every spark of hope, knowing his love could never be fulfilled. He had risen to the position of overseer of the extensive seigniory, taken his meals with the family, and in all respects enjoyed the elevated treatment offered by the Bilivertis.

Then when the marchese had proposed his betrothal to Anabella, the shock of the reversal of his fortunes had completely overwhelmed him. He had readily agreed, following the emotions of his heart rather than the sound judgment of his mind.

Back in the present, Albret sighed with internal turmoil. To be worthy of her, he needed to be of the upper class, also a man of courage and honor. Yet now he was engaged in a battle against this privileged class, so tainted with dishonor and intrigue. The Turatis and the Bilivertis were exceptions, secretly supporting the poor and disadvantaged. Surely the marchese would understand why after careful reflection he must withdraw from their agreement—the man might even be grateful.

&

Sunday afternoon when the castle occupants had returned from services, Albret and the marchese, Anabella's brother, sat on stone benches in the castle's inner courtyard. Albret had just painfully explained his reasons for withdrawing the agreement to betroth Anabella. Silence hung between the two men. Albret tried to swallow but found his mouth dry.

Suddenly the marchese stood and paced in front of him. "I do understand your desire to rise in the world—and you will do so, a man of your ability and knowledge. Well, you and Anabella are both still young. I considered several men with titles and lands before I realized you were the best choice for my sister. Mother and I noticed that you treated her with the utmost respect and showed an interest in her life. And she loves you. Unless that has changed?" His voice was steady and seemed devoid of anger.

"No, Marchese, I don't believe her feelings. . .for me. . .have changed," Albret said, not entirely convinced himself. He stood as he addressed his friend and master. Though his arm was bound to his body by bandages, he knew he cut a handsome figure. Yet he felt the fashionable doublet, hosen, and dress boots served as a disguise, presenting a man he was not. "I could accept the traditional dowry, but while you have been most generous in offering to build us a villa and grant us a portion of your estate, that is what a husband needs to provide. And Anabella can only be happy in an elegant villa—which is beyond my means."

"She said that?" The two men walked down the graveled path edged by clipped hedges and drying flowers of autumn.

"Not exactly," Albret said with hesitation.

"Frankly, Albret Maseo, I am disappointed in this decision. I believe you are making a grave error." With that, the marchese hastened his gait and entered the castle, leaving Albret alone to contemplate the results of his actions.

¾

The marchese spent the next few days away from the castle, negotiating a purchase of horses. Albret was thus left to complete his recovery under the tender care of his mother and Bianca. He had been stung by the marchese's words of reproof and was eager to return to the front, yet he found great pleasure in the Bilivertis' young son, Pietro, who was just learning to walk.

He and the Marchesa Bianca sat opposite each other on a woven rug in the salon. As childhood friends, he felt this relationship still intact, despite his growing unease with class distinction. The two encouraged little Pietro to toddle between them. Albret reached out both arms, as indeed the wound had sufficiently healed, to catch the baby just as he completed a dozen steps or so.

"That's the first time he's made it all the way without tripping!" His mother beamed with pride. "Albret, the baby has brought so much pleasure to our lives."

"I can see that," said Albret with a smile. "Who wouldn't love such a beautiful, healthy child? For whom is he named?"

"My grandfather Pietro Marinelli." Albret saw a shadow pass across her face as from a deep sadness.

"He left Milan as a young man, taking my grandmother and their two little boys—one of whom became my father."

Little Pietro curled up in Albret's lap and tugged on his shirt.

"Shirt," said Albret.

"Sert," repeated Pietro.

Bianca smiled in admiration and continued her story. "The wars in Milan destroyed his business, so he took his family to France. There they found some success in farming. Unfortunately, civil war broke out in that country also. He was a very religious man and felt God wished him to befriend any refugees from the war that came his way. The government arrested him for sheltering Huguenots—and he died in prison."

"I'm so sorry," said Albret, stroking the curls of the child, who yawned and snuggled in his arms.

"Of course, I didn't know him, but I heard the family story many times. I wanted to honor his memory. I'm not sure war ever betters people's lives."

"I will do what I can to bring a better life to the peasants," Albret promised. He handed Bianca the sleepy baby.

"There is no glory in fighting," she said as she hugged the child and placed him in his cradle.

Albret kept his silence. He felt weak and disadvantaged, recuperating from battle wounds in the elegant home of his childhood friend—a home where he no longer belonged. *Is it not honorable to shed blood, or even to die, for a noble purpose?*

five

Anabella rushed from the room where she had been tutoring the orphan boys, clutching the letter Papa Antonio had just handed her. Could there be some word about Albret? In her room, Anabella fell into an upholstered chair and with anxious fingers broke the seal of the letter from her brother, Marco. She read:

Dear 'Bella,

I trust you and Mother are well. Our news of the rebellion is delayed and often not dependable as it is, for the most part, filtered through our neighbors, the Bargerinos, who do not agree with the peasants' cause. Bianca and I take a neutral stance—though we have allowed a few of our workers to fight alongside their peers.

However, we—as well as Sylvia—have seen the unfortunate results of fighting. Our trusted Massetti retrieved by carriage your dear Albret from the battlefield. Don't be alarmed. He suffered a sword wound to his upper arm but is now nearly restored to his robust health. He left this morning to return to his squadron, and I presume is still fighting near Siena.

Albret informed me of your broken betrothal, which much distresses me. He assured me that he loves no other but you, and I believe him. His decision, he asserts, solely concerns what he considers his unworthiness to provide for you honorably and well.

I recall that year in Rome when we were temporarily deposed from our castle and status. That was a frightening time for you as a child, and I do not desire for you ever to be reduced to that state again. Albret's pride pushes him to refuse the security of the gift I have offered to both of you—a villa and lands.

For now, I have left intact the impalmare, recorded in the church two years ago, stating both parties' intentions and the financial agreements. Please be assured, my dear sister, that your happiness is of utmost importance to me.

Though I am responsible for making decisions on your behalf in the absence of our dear, deceased father, I will consider your feelings. Do you still love this man? Shall I leave the impalmare unchanged? Do you want me to charge him with breach of promise? Please inform me of your wishes.

Bianca and little Pietro send their love along with mine.

Marco

Wounded, my Albret wounded? Anabella reread the letter, folded it, and lay it aside. She had tried not to think of him. Now emotion surged through her body. What if he were to die? What if she never saw him again? *What shall I tell Marco?*

She made her way to the private family chapel. A small round window of stained glass depicting the Madonna and Child let sunlight fall in varied colors across the altar. She knelt on the white satin cushion and prayed, "Lord Jesus, keep Albret in perfect peace and out of harm. Bring us together again, if it be Thy will."

She knew then what she must do. In her stepfather's study she found paper and quills. She wrote:

Dearest Marco,

I love Albret with all my heart. Please do not yet rescind our impalmare, and do not bring charges against him. I have placed our future in God's hands and trust Him to bring what is right to pass.

Your loving sister,
Anabella

She folded the paper, dripped wax on it, and impressed

it with the Turati seal. She would have it delivered with her mother's next letter to Marco. But Albret had already returned to battle. How would *he* know her feelings?

The next morning, Anabella's thoughts continued to linger on her concern for Albret, but the autumnal ball at the Strozzi Palace would take place that night. The day could only be dedicated to preparation. With mixed emotions, she bound lace to the scooped neckline of a lavender silk gown with puffed sleeves, which she had designed and created for this special occasion. The Soderini sisters had both praised her artistry and suggested she put her hair up to appear more mature. Shortly, Luisa would braid it and wind it into a bun on the crown of her head in the style worn by most Florentine women.

Just yesterday she had written her brother that she loved Albret. And she did. Yet she anticipated meeting young nobles at the ball with decided curiosity. She had made few friends in the two years since she and her mother moved to Florence. And Cecilia and Simonetta had promised to introduce her to a conte of superior reputation.

❧

Anabella arrived with her parents in an elaborately carved and painted carriage pulled by four white stallions. A personal servant accompanied each family member. Clarice had been with her mother for years. Giorgio served Papa Antonio, and Luisa came with Anabella. The latter two were among the street orphans the family had taken to their villa to nurture and train. For these young people, it was their first encounter with Florentine social life, and their eyes shown with bright excitement.

A groomsman met them at the gate to take their carriage and horses. Another servant escorted them to the entrance, and still another announced their arrival to their hosts and guests. A house servant bowed low and took the ladies' capes. The Strozzi couple warmly welcomed the family and whisked away Anabella's mother and stepfather.

Simonetta arrived on the arm of her escort. "Anabella, I am delighted you have come," she said. "This is Visconte Carlo Strozzi. Carlo, please meet my dearest friend, Anabella Biliverti, daughter of the former Marchesa Costanza Biliverti, now the *Baronessa* Turati. Her father was the late Marchese Lorenzino Biliverti of Terni, and her stepfather is the renowned Barone Antonio Turati."

As her stepfather rarely used his purchased title, Anabella assumed Simonetta did so to impress her visconte.

"A distinct pleasure, my dear," said the visconte with a bow as he took and kissed her hand.

"The pleasure is mine," said Anabella, smiling.

"I do want you to meet someone you will find charming," said Simonetta, taking Anabella's hand and leading her through the crowd, the visconte following. They found the conte in the ballroom admiring a painting of fruit and flowers by the late Caravaggio.

The conte turned toward them as they approached. Anabella had expected an older man, but he appeared only in his mid-twenties. Indeed, he was handsome and charming, tall, broad shouldered, and sporting a pointed beard and black mustache that curled upward at the ends.

With a wide smile, he took Anabella's hand in both of his. Looking directly into her eyes—and deeply into her very soul as well, she felt—he said, "You grow more beautiful each time we meet, Anabella. The color lavender enhances those lovely eyes."

Intrigued by his manner, she found herself at a loss for words. But she did not fail to notice a cut just above his right wrist, healing but of recent origin.

"Do you two know each other?" asked Simonetta, surprised at his remark.

"No, I don't believe—"

"Ah, but yes, my dear," the conte said, running his fingers through his black, wavy locks. "Let me think. I danced with you—"

"Are you the Bargerino cousin? And have now become a conte?"

"Yes. And yes. My father died last year and left me the title and lands," he said without showing any sign of grief. "I remember now. We first met when you were a mere child. A ball at the Biliverti castle in Terni. Your father was still living."

"Yes, we had many delightful social events at the castle then," she said wistfully.

"And again we danced at my relatives' carnival ball two or three years ago. It must have been two, because I spent most of that summer on their estate in Terni."

"Yes, I do remember. You are Frederico Bargerino," she said with a winsome smile. "Conte Bargerino."

"To you, I will always simply be Frederico."

Cecilia appeared and introduced her escort, Romolo, the Barone di Bicci. He, too, was handsome—though shorter and somewhat stout—and wore his beard and mustache in identical fashion to the conte's. Frederico tucked Anabella's arm under his, and the three couples headed to the banquet hall. Alas, she was seated next to her parents, and Frederico sat at a different table surrounded by other young women but obscured from her view.

Anabella did recall that night of the carnival ball. Albret had been invited due to his recent promotion to overseer. Whereas he proved to be a strong leader among men, he had never danced before and thus lingered most of the evening alone in dark corners. She, however, never missed a dance. Frederico was only one of many young men who had vied for her attention that night. Later she had regretted abandoning her friend Albret, and to make up for her neglect, she tutored him on the popular dance steps in their own ballroom.

The seven-course banquet drew to a close, and the fifty or so guests filed to the ballroom. Anabella left her reverie and followed her parents. An ensemble of stringed instruments struck up the music of a suite in the new rococo mode, and the dancing began. Papa Antonio took her mother in his arms and disappeared into the crowd, leaving Anabella standing alone, save for the family attendants nearby.

She wished Albret could be at her side, but instead, Conte Frederico suddenly appeared. He placed his hand on her elbow and whispered, "May I be honored by the first dance with you, dear lady?"

Flattered by his attentions, Anabella allowed him to take her hand and lead her to the floor. Her concerns about Albret— his battle wounds and their broken betrothal—faded as she swirled about the room in the conte's arms. A man of apparent cultured tastes, he conversed on every subject from architecture to art to the new musical form called opera. No other young man dared to break into his monopoly of her.

Abruptly, he changed the topic of conversation to a more personal one. "By the way, who was that boy who accompanied you to the carnival ball in Terni that night? He seemed shy, and you never danced with him. But I saw you leave together with your mother."

"Oh, that would have been Albret Maseo," she said, shocked that he would have remembered him—or even taken notice.

"And how is he related to the Bilivertis? Your cousin perhaps?"

"Albret is not—"

"Excuse me, my dear, I must speak to someone." Still holding her hand, he tapped the shoulder of his host, Signore Strozzi, who was just leading his wife from the floor between dances. After a few words and nodding by both men, Frederico turned back to her and said, "Please, forgive me. I shall return shortly." He led her to a velvet-upholstered settee beneath a Botticelli painting, bowed with a light kiss to her hand, and slipped back through the crowd.

Within a few minutes, the visconte deposited Simonetta beside her. "I believe the conte is strongly attracted to you," she said with a knowing twinkle in her eye.

"Do you think so? I do find him rather charming." She smiled and dabbed her damp forehead with a lace handkerchief. "I'm glad to have a pause from the dancing. I thought he was rather brusque, however, in suddenly deciding he had to talk to our host."

"He's soliciting funds for his cause. Didn't you know?"

Before Anabella could answer, the visconte retrieved Simonetta, and she was left alone until a gentleman approached and asked her for the next dance. She politely refused, claiming fatigue. It was sufficient to sit and take in the extravagant decor of the ballroom, all with an eye for her own decorative design. But she wondered, *What cause? What funds?*

six

With only hearsay reports in Terni to guide him, Albret rode with two saddlebags of supplies strapped across his horse, searching for the field of battle. From Biliverti servants who had talked with Bargerino servants, he'd heard that the conte's troops had beaten back the peasants and forced them to give up their "ridiculous cause."

Yet as he neared Siena, peasant women along the road informed him that their husbands and sons were fighting valiantly on. Late in the day, he passed burned fields and the abandoned debris of battle. He considered whether to hide out and continue his journey in the morning or ride on with caution until he approached the battle scene. The latter seemed more to his nature, though he knew how vulnerable a single soldier would be to attack. With eyes and ears alert, he spurred his horse onward, facing the sun as it lowered in the western sky.

A sound in the forest beside the road startled him. Halting his steed, he listened. Concluding it must have been only a deer bounding through the underbrush, he rode on. Then came sounds of human activity—the clank of a kettle, the mumbling of voices. He tied his horse to a sapling secluded from view on the other side of the road and crept stealthily toward the sounds. Friend or foe?

Leaning against a large oak tree, he peered around it. Immediately, the dress and paltry accommodations of the troops told him he had arrived at his destination. Exhaling with relief, he approached the troops, who were in various stages of finishing their evening meal, cleaning up, and preparing to leave.

"Ho, Albret!" said one. "I'm glad you survived your wounds.

We need you, and Captain Gaza asks about you every day."

"Well, I am here and eager to speak with him. I hear all sorts of rumors. How goes the battle, my good man?"

Several hands offered him meat and drink, which he consumed, noticing neither substance nor taste. The men crowded about him, all vying to tell the story.

"They beat us terribly about ten days ago. . ."

"Burned our camp, slaughtered our men. . ."

"They thought we couldn't recover—that we'd lost our will."

"The conte even sent his messenger to dictate terms. Said King Philip had been informed of our disloyal rebellion and would send Spanish troops to murder us all if we didn't go back to our homes and live in peace."

"As if we had homes to go back to. It's the conte who is forcing us off the land where our ancestors lived and worked."

"So we scoffed at the messenger and sent him back to tell the conte that 'glory and honor belong to the valiant,' meaning us, and 'right is on our side.'"

"Where do I report to Captain Gaza?" asked Albret, stirred by the peasants' enthusiasm.

"He is still camped with the B Division. We are to wait here for orders but are to be prepared to move," said a fellow who pointed to the north. Albret retrieved his horse and rode down the path.

Albret found the captain outside his tent talking with Massetti. Both men looked up with surprise and warmly welcomed him with handshakes. Massetti quickly dismissed himself, and Captain Gaza invited Albret to sit with him on overturned buckets. Only a few men remained in the deserted camp, rolling up tents and packing away equipment. A chill hung in the still air after the setting of the sun.

"I thank God, you are back, Albret. Many of our wounded have not returned, but I see you have recovered. Strong as ever?"

"Yes, signore. I am eager to serve at your pleasure."

"Good. We strike before dawn. I need you to lead the

A Division. After the massacre—as that's all you can call it—many of the conte's mercenaries, who had received their pay, returned home. Some of the noblemen who served as officers also considered the battle over and left. Those who remained encamped across the river and have not ceased to celebrate their victory with wine and song—even after their messenger returned to tell them we would fight on. Our spies have observed it all."

"So we will strike from two fronts?"

"Exactly," said Captain Gaza with a glint in his eye that Albret could not miss even in the fading light. "As you see, we are now well armed. Before, we had run out of gunpowder and even food. An esteemed barone from Florence—who, of course, must keep his name secret—has supplied a tremendous amount of ammunition and other necessities, as well as a cannon."

"Wonderful!" exclaimed Albret. "But how can we drag a cannon into position without being detected?"

"Well, since the cannon came from Florence to the north, they brought it up the far side of the hill where our B Division has been camped for two days. Thus our enemy is unknowingly trapped between that hill and the river."

"Good strategy," said Albret, rubbing his clean-shaven chin. "And the other division?"

"That's where you come in. There is a little-used stone bridge that spans the river south of the enemy encampment. The road that leads to it is overgrown with weeds and brush. I will cross over this night on horseback to lead the division already on the hilltop. After our overpowering onslaught from there, the enemy will retreat and attempt to escape across the bridge. There is an open area on this side of it. We will allow most of them to cross and take their repose. Then we blow up the bridge as the last of their troops scramble across."

"Brilliant," said Albret. "Then we in the A Division attack the enemy in repose?"

"That is correct. Massetti has the map and explosives. You

will lead the division and lie in wait at the edge of the forest. A shot from the cannon—well before sunup—will announce that the attack has commenced."

&

Anabella, still aglow from Frederico's flattery, hummed a tune from the previous evening as she prepared coffee for her stepfather and his guest. It was a relatively new beverage for which Papa Antonio had acquired a taste while in Rome. Though she did not share his enthusiasm for it, she had learned to brew it to his liking. She placed a small pitcher of warm milk on the tray next to the steaming cups and carried it all to the salon.

Papa Antonio sat facing the door, but his guest, to whom he spoke, sat opposite him, blocking his view. He was thus unaware of her entrance.

She waited, not wishing to interrupt such intense discourse.

"But Paolo, I have already donated a cannon to the cause along with six balls, gunpowder, and other supplies. That is simply all I can do. I have my reputation, as do you. We could lose valuable clients if we showed our hand."

"I understand, Signore Turati. But if the peasants are victorious, as I believe they will be, they will need an articulate spokesman to negotiate with the king's emissaries in Madrid."

"You could fulfill the role as well as I, but—"

"That's doubtful."

"It doesn't matter. My name is still associated with the merchandising train that you will be running. If I were involved, it would reflect upon you. All I can offer is to try to think of someone—ah, Anabella, do come in."

"*Caffè latte!*" said Paolo with exuberance. "And how pleasant to see you again, my dear."

"The pleasure is mine, signore," she said with a friendly smile, setting the tray on a table between the two men. She bowed slightly and made a quick exit.

Her parents rarely shared news about the conflict, claiming

they wished to shield her from violent reality. She knew by custom that someone her age would not be privy to such news, but she resented being shut out of a situation that involved Albret. Although she had shared Marco's letter and her response with her mother, both parents seemed unaware of her keen interest in events.

If they are talking about negotiation, then the struggle must be near an end. She donned a cape and went out in the courtyard to watch the sun set. So many questions troubled her mind as she paced the graveled walkways. The lower edges of gray clouds gradually turned to brilliant purple, red, and gold as the sun sank lower. The thrill of dancing in the arms of the conte lost all significance. *I wonder if Albret is watching this sunset? Or is he engaged in battle at this very moment? Fighting to the—no I cannot think that word.* She covered her face with her hands and wept.

&

The troops in the A Division waited in the dark of a moonless night. Albret insisted they catch some sleep as the time of the cannon blast was uncertain. There would be plenty of time to prepare to intercept the fleeing enemy troops as they crossed the bridge into the open field. However, the peasants knew this to be their last stand. If defeated here, they could only go home in shame, and their fallen brothers would have died in vain.

Albret's new responsibility of commanding troops weighed heavily on his shoulders. This was different from organizing and directing groups of workers—here every decision carried with it a life or death outcome.

Albret, Massetti, and the guards stood watch. As stars grew dimmer, he began to worry that the B Division had waited too late for the surprise attack. He paced at the edge of the forest and looked out over the still, open space, devoid of activity. He could detect a sheet of fog that hung in the cool, damp air. That would serve to their advantage, hiding them from the enemy until the last minute.

Boom! The sound seemed to crack open the earth. The troops sprang to their feet and stood ready, their hands eagerly fingering their guns or daggers. At Albret's command, two trusted soldiers crept silently through the dead weeds, tied the explosives to the bridge, and lay silently in the shadows to ignite the explosives at the right moment. Albret mounted his horse. The animal pawed the ground in anticipation. Gunfire echoed from across the river.

An hour passed. Sounds of guns firing continued. Albret finally heard the sixth cannon blast. He knew that would be the last. Silence. Then the thundering roar of horses galloping across the bridge. He could see their gray silhouettes dispersing into the open place. There, fatigued from battle, they dismounted and dropped their guard.

A powerful explosion lit up the sky. The enemy turned to stare in shocked disbelief. Flames leaped up from the bridge, catching on small trees and shrubs.

"Charge!" shouted Albret and led on horseback with his sword pointed skyward.

His men, mostly on foot, rushed to attack from the rear. Few of the conte's men had time to remount their steeds; thus they were forced to meet the ambush on equal footing. Swords and daggers clashed. Gunfire crackled. The dead and wounded fell.

From his advantage on horseback, Albret slashed at the enemy still on foot. Then suddenly, three mounted men rode directly toward him, firing pistols—peasant soldiers dropping away on either side. For the first time in battle, fear of his own death gripped him. He turned his horse sideways and slipped off his saddle on the unexposed side just as bullets riddled the animal.

As the horse fell, Albret sprang up and lunged with his sword toward the last of the passing gunmen. He knocked him from his steed, wrenched his weapon from him, and squeezed the trigger. Alas, it was void of gunpowder. His foe grabbed the hilt of a sword that hung from his side and faced Albret.

The man screamed obscenities and charged toward him. The two men fought until Albret attacked with a swift blow to the side of his enemy's head, sending him sprawling to the ground. Albret mounted his foe's horse and rode off to assist his countrymen in the western part of the battlefield.

An hour later as the sun rose in the eastern sky, the peasants claimed victory. The remnant of the enemy rushed to the river's edge, but alas, if they swam across, more armed, shouting peasants awaited them on the other side. Albret left them to their fate and returned to help gather his dead and wounded into wagons.

None of the defeated attempted to follow the victorious as they trudged back to the appointed camp. The peasants would need to wait a full day before their other division could join them in celebration.

"Did anyone see the conte?" asked Albret as he walked along beside the absconded horse that carried a wounded man.

Among the knowing laughter of several, Massetti said, "That craven man? He's probably hiding with his private guards. He rarely enters the fray unless he has the advantage."

"Is that so?" Albret savored this delicious information as it paralleled his own conclusion.

ॐ

Three days later after the victory celebration, the burial of the dead, and the tending to the wounded, the peasants sat in small groups discussing the possible results of their successful rebellion. It was late afternoon, and storm clouds were rolling in. Albret sat with Captain Gaza, Massetti, and a few others, each recounting his personal story from his point in the battle.

"What do we do now, Captain?" asked Massetti.

"I see a lone man on horseback bearing a white flag," said the captain, shading his eyes. "Perhaps he brings us our answer."

Albret and Massetti followed his gaze. The man dismounted when he arrived in front of them.

"I come in peace," said the messenger through tense lips. He pulled a letter from inside his doublet and, looking over the three men, handed it to the captain. "This is from my master, Conte Bargerino. I will wait a distance away if you wish to send a reply." He tipped his hat. "Captain Gaza."

"Yes, please wait, signore," said the captain. When the messenger was out of earshot, he turned to Albret. "Would you be so kind as to read this aloud?"

Brilliant in battle as the captain had proved himself, Albret guessed that his formal education had been sparse. "Certainly, signore." He read:

> *Captain Gaza:*
>
> *You may have beaten us to retreat on the battlefront, but a far better means of settling disputes is diplomacy. Therefore, I have sent word to King Philip's court in Madrid, requesting that he set a date for arbitration. Do you agree to send a representative to present your complaints? And do you agree, without further warfare, to abide by the decision of the king's representative?*
>
> *We wish to consider my right to make decisions concerning my own inherited property and the people who live thereon; the right of the king to continue to require citizens to donate a month of labor in building the roads of the kingdom; and the right of the king to levy taxes of his choosing on the citizens of Italy.*
>
> *As I am a generous man, I offer you this opportunity to let your grievances be heard before the king's emissaries.*
>
> *My messenger will await your reply.*
> *Conte Frederico Bargerino*

The captain's immediate reaction was to slap his knee and guffaw loudly. "Ha! What a sly way to admit total defeat! Diplomacy is exactly what we proposed at the beginning, and he refused. Massetti, please fetch paper, quill, and ink from my tent."

As soon as Massetti left, the captain became quite somber, leaned toward Albret, and whispered, "Albret, I know what to ask for but do not have the words to present a case and argue the points."

"But Captain, you have right on your side."

"True, but in situations like this, I am a poor spokesman. Without your brave and heroic leadership, we might have lost this fight. I am now asking you to battle in the same manner with words, to go before the king's emissaries as my representative—the representative of the people. I will choose a small staff to accompany us."

"I will consider this." Albret felt honored but totally inadequate for such an awesome task.

"There is no time to consider. The messenger is waiting. There is Massetti now with paper and quill. Please—for your countrymen."

"I will do as you ask, Captain."

"I thank you. Your country thanks you." Suddenly the captain again became buoyant. "Thank you, Massetti. And now, Albret, please write as I dictate."

"Certainly, Captain." Albret took the writing material.

"But first I must tell you, Albret, that you are to leave immediately after penning this." A gust of wind fluttered the paper in Albret's hand. "Report to the villa of a certain barone this side of Florence. He is a business associate of the anonymous merchant whom you contacted before. In fact, I've learned that this barone is the person who supplied the cannon and other ammunition for this last assault. You will find his estate just past the village of Impruneta. Arrangements have already been made for you to spend a few days there while his tailor outfits you appropriately for your mission. I will call for you there."

"As you wish, Captain."

"His name is Barone Antonio Turati."

seven

Papa Antonio had gone into Florence for a few days to consult with Paolo, his friend and business associate. Both Anabella and her mother assumed the meeting concerned the transfer of his merchandise train to Paolo. But Anabella did recall that the two had discussed the peasant rebellion and the need for someone to negotiate on the peasants' behalf.

Anabella spent her mornings tutoring the orphans her family had taken in. Ordinarily she began with the boys, coaching them in reading, spelling, and writing. Her mother would then take over with a Bible lesson and some geography. Papa Antonio taught science and history, followed in the afternoon by horsemanship and husbandry.

Recently she and her mother had begun to instruct three girls in domestic skills, etiquette, and reading. Papa Antonio had rescued poor Luisa from being sold into prostitution. At sixteen she was a year older than Anabella, but because of her small size and shyness, she appeared younger. The other two were sisters about ten and eleven years old whose mother had abandoned them to their grandmother. The grandmother had died and left them to the streets. This morning Anabella held their class in an open alcove by the staircase. She had given each girl a sampler to embroider.

"Now watch as I make this stitch. Pull the thread through, then loop back under thus," said Anabella with all the patience in the world. "Fine, excellent. Now continue. No, this way. Make the stitch, then insert the needle. . ."

"Like this, signorina?" questioned Luisa.

Anabella looked up to see Giorgio approaching. With a slight bow, he handed her an embossed envelope.

"What's this, Giorgio?"

"A messenger just delivered it to Signora Turati during our class. She asked that I bring it here, signorina, as it is addressed to you."

Her heart pounded rapidly as she thought it might be from Albret, but alas, she knew he would not have sent such an ornate missive from the battlefront. *Perhaps it's a notice that he's been wounded again, or worse. . .*

"Please, excuse me a moment, girls. Yes, Luisa, that is correct. Continue as I showed you." The seal had already been broken—no doubt by her protective mother. Slowly she removed the contents. She felt three pairs of curious eyes watching her, but she was too focused to care. Silently she read:

> *To the Signorina Anabella Biliverti,*
> *Conte Frederico Bargerino requests the honor of accompanying you to a private presentation of the opera* Dafne *by Jacopo Peri in the Corsi Palace where it was first performed in 1597. The hosts expect around thirty guests.*
> *The* conte *will call for you in his carriage, 3 October at seven of the clock. His messenger awaits at the gates for your response.*
>
> > *With all due respect and affection, the* conte *remains*
> > *Your devoted,*
> > *Frederico*

Anabella closed her eyes and sighed, adjusting her emotions from concern for Albret to the flattering offer from the fascinating conte.

"I am to await your response, signorina," said Giorgio, who had discretely stepped aside. "Signora Turati says to tell you that you are free to make your own choice—about which I am not privy."

"Thank you, Giorgio." She pulled her lace handkerchief from her sleeve but found no purpose for it other than to twist it thoughtfully. "Tell the messenger, Giorgio, that. . .that Signorina Biliverti accepts his kind offer with pleasure."

With only two days to prepare, Anabella felt rushed. In truth, she acknowledged a bit of resentment that the invitation had come so late, as if an afterthought. *Perhaps he asked another first who has refused him.* Nevertheless, an invitation from the dashing and charming conte interested her. She had never attended one of these new genres of entertainment, combining drama and music. However, Papa Antonio had spoken with great admiration of Monteverdi's *L'Orfeo*, which he had witnessed in Rome.

❧

Anabella donned a beige satin gown with a burgundy velvet inset in the bodice and a split overskirt of the same material. It was not new, for she had worn it to the wedding of her mother and Papa Antonio, but she felt it made her appear maturer. Luisa braided her hair and formed a bun high on the back of her head. She bound it with a wide velvet ribbon. Dark ringlets fell softly at the sides of her face. Her mother loaned her a necklace with an opal pendant and reminded her of the rules of etiquette that a young signorina must follow on such occasions.

Her mother's personal servant, Clarice, who would accompany her as chaperone, tapped on Anabella's bedroom door and announced the arrival of Conte Bargerino. They descended the staircase and found him and his personal manservant waiting in the entrance hall.

The conte, dressed all in black save the narrow white ruff of a collar, took her hand and bowed with all the grace of a gentleman, sweeping his plumed hat in front of himself. His polished dress sword hung at his side. After a few polite words of reassurance to her mother—who stood anxiously behind her—he took her arm, and they set off.

In the carriage, Frederico—for indeed, that is what he insisted she call him—explained the format and content of the opera they would see. "The story of *Dafne*," he said, "comes from Greek mythology. Daphne, you see, was the daughter of a river god. According to the myth, Apollo was pursuing her when her mother changed her into a laurel tree. The purpose of course was for her daughter's protection against the powerful god."

Anabella found his tone condescending; nevertheless, she looked up at him and smiled. "I see," she said.

The evening proved to be delightful. Anabella enjoyed the instrumental music and the trained voices of the performers, and afterward she mingled easily among the guests, goblet in hand, making new acquaintances. She had never before met any of these people, as not even the Soderini sisters had been invited.

In truth, she remembered the story of Daphne from her tutoring in Greek myths, but she remained silent as her escort explained to her its symbolism in simple terms and discussed the merits of the new genre with the other guests. He seemed to delight in doing so.

The few times, however, that she left his side, she detected whisperings among the guests that included smirks and glances toward the conte. The words she picked up—"angry peasants" and "battleground"—confused her further, as they could have in no way applied to him. *He is not involved in the peasant rebellion.* But their comments directly to the conte all concerned their favorable impressions of her as his new companion. She reveled in the flattery.

The carriage arrived back at the villa just before midnight. As a rainstorm threatened, the conte quickly bid her goodnight at the door with the words, "All eyes were on you tonight, my beautiful Anabella, and I felt proud to introduce you to my sphere of influence. You will hear from me again soon." He bowed and released her to Clarice's keeping.

As Anabella crawled into bed that night, the pounding rain began in earnest. She spent a restless night, sleep evading her as she tossed about, troubled—yet not understanding why—over the meaning of the conte's words to her as well as the element of gossip about him. Certainly, he was a gentleman in every way. Certainly, he continually showered her with compliments. She enjoyed his attention and that of the other guests. The opera had been magical, so she tried to concentrate on it.

Suddenly the image of Albret came to the fore—almost like a vision in her half-asleep state. He smiled at her and touched the hilt of his sword. She reached her arms out to him and called his name. "Not yet, my love," he whispered and faded into the darkness.

Will I ever see my true love again? she wondered. She squeezed her eyes shut and imagined the warmth of his nearness. Finally, sleep came just as cocks began to crow.

Later that morning when she awoke, it was the image of Albret that remained with her rather than thoughts of an exciting evening with the conte. Albret was still on her mind as the family broke their fast. To all her mother's questions about the previous evening, Anabella distractedly answered, "The conte is a perfect gentleman."

"And is the conte someone with whom you might like to spend your future?"

The question shocked her into focus. "What, Mother?" she responded with an edge to her voice.

"Conte Frederico Bargerino. Would he be suitable for consideration as your husband? Of course that is for your brother, Marco, to decide, but—"

"Mother, you know Marco has not rescinded the impalmare agreement. I am left hanging between it and the withdrawal of our intended betrothal. But you also know Albret is the man I love. I do not seek another. Frankly, in answer to your question, I feel uneasy with the conte." She spoke gently, though the words were decisive, then pushed back her breakfast plate and rose to go. "I will be in the chapel, Mother."

At that moment, Papa Antonio strode into room looking jovial. After hanging his damp cloak on a hook by the kitchen, he poured himself a cup of coffee and sat down beside his wife. He kissed her on the forehead. "Well, ladies, I have a bit of news."

Anabella returned to her seat and folded her hands on the table.

"You've concluded your new business arrangement with Paolo?" said her mother, kissing him on the cheek.

"No. Well, yes, we did sign papers. I am the silent partner with only a third interest now, Costanza." He smiled at Anabella and reached across the table, placing his hand on hers. "But my news concerns a certain Albret Maseo."

Anabella's hand flinched. "He's not been killed?"

"No, no, my dear. The peasants have beaten back the conte and his mercenaries and emerged victorious. I understand that Albret led the charge. The conte has acknowledged defeat and requested arbitration from King Philip."

"That is, indeed, good news," said her mother, buttering a chunk of bread and setting it before her husband. "I am so glad the fighting is over. And Albret will be returning to Terni?"

"Not yet."

Papa Antonio's words seemed to resound in her head. *Not yet, my love,* Albret had whispered when she reached her arms out for him in her dream.

"Albret will be coming here first," he continued. "The captain of the troops has asked Albret to be his representative before the king's emissaries to present their cause."

"Albret is coming here!" exclaimed Anabella, feeling extremely proud and, for a moment, forgetting that anything had changed between them. "That is a weighty responsibility for him. But he will present the case well; I am sure of it."

"Albret is articulate and knowledgeable. We can all be proud that he was chosen for the prestigious role. He will bring honor to himself and the peasant cause," said her stepfather.

"Honor?" breathed Anabella.

"He should arrive here in time for the evening meal, so we will 'kill the fatted calf,' so to speak," said Papa Antonio. "My tailor will make a proper outfit for him to wear on this venture to Madrid. Thus he will remain here a few days."

Anabella felt her heart beat wildly with excitement, but she dared not ask questions. This was, indeed, more information than Papa Antonio usually shared with her.

All morning, Anabella found it difficult to concentrate on her instructions to the children, so nervous was she about seeing Albret. By early afternoon, the rain had stopped, and sun shone through the stained glass of the chapel where she paged through the large Bible that lay open on a stand. She found Psalm 46 and read the words of assurance that she remembered were contained in verse 9: "He maketh wars to cease unto the end of the earth; he breaketh the bow, and cutteth the spear in sunder."

She knelt in prayer and thanked God for delivering Albret in battle. After she learned he had been wounded, she had asked for God's protection over Albret, and not only had he been spared, but the Lord had delivered the enemy into his hands. And now he had been given a daunting task.

She rose and returned to the Bible that remained open to the psalm. She read it from beginning to end: "God is our refuge and strength, a very present help in trouble. . . The Lord of hosts is with us: the God of Jacob is our refuge."

"Lord God, I claim Your promises that You will always be with us and Your assurance that we can find our strength in You. Please be with Albret as he goes to speak before the king's emissaries. Give him the words to say. And be with both of us when we meet, for we have become estranged one from the other." With calmness and assurance, she left the chapel to prepare for Albret's arrival.

She bathed and selected a simple, light blue dress with white lace cuffs. Declining any help from Luisa, Anabella brushed her hair and tied it back at the nape of her neck with a blue ribbon and let her natural curls frame her face. *No need to pretend this will be a romantic evening. His mind will be set on the task ahead.* But she placed a dab of rose water behind each ear.

Entering the salon, she became alarmed upon hearing the voices of her mother and Papa Antonio. They stood facing each other and seemed to be quite upset about something. She had never heard them argue, and indeed, that did not appear to be the case now.

When her stepfather noticed her, he quickly changed his tone. "Ah, Anabella, you look lovely, my dear. Dinner preparations are near completion, and we only await the arrival of Albret. I will go check on 'the fatted calf.' "

"Actually, it's a roasted goose," her mother said with a forced little laugh.

The redness around her mother's eyes betrayed the light-hearted comment.

"What is the matter, Mother?" asked Anabella, placing an arm around her.

"Nothing. Nothing at all, Daughter," she said as she seated herself on one of the brocaded chairs.

Anabella took an adjacent chair. *Nothing* simply meant the topic was not meant for her young ears. As a dutiful child, she would not pursue the issue further.

"However, Anabella, I have been meaning to return to a subject I brought up just this morning." She drew a handkerchief from her sleeve and blotted the corners of her eyes.

"Yes, Mother, go on."

"Do you recall what I asked you about Conte Bargerino?"

"Of course. You asked if I would consider him as a potential husband. Forgive me, Mother, for so quickly dismissing the idea. I'm sure he would make a fine husband. Although I respect your wishes, I am just not ready to think in those terms. Not yet."

"I understand fully. We really know so little about him. I was basing my thoughts on what we know about his relatives, the Bargerinos of Terni. Your father and I always held them in high esteem. They are honest people and fair to their workers. Antonio never had an opportunity to meet them before we married and moved here. We just know nothing about this Frederico. . ."

"Nor do I, Mother," she said, recalling the evening at the opera. "Other than he is handsome, charming, and knowledgeable on many topics." She recalled the instances of the guests apparently gossiping about him when his back was turned. "He is a gentleman."

"Yes, Anabella, you told me that several times this morning." Her mother managed to put a smile on her tearstained face. "I am just withdrawing my suggestion. You need not concern yourself further about it. Let's go pull Antonio from the kitchen. Before our marriage, he was worse than a housewife—always peeking in the ovens and stirring the pots. In fact, he did much of his own cooking."

"I know, Mother." She took her mother's hand, and together they headed toward the kitchen.

eight

Anabella sat across from Albret at the dinner table, enthralled by his every word. He spoke rapidly with excitement as he recounted the details of the final assault on the enemy. The young man was not wont to boast, but Anabella felt he had made an exception for her benefit. She cherished hearing the details of his exploits.

"I've not eaten so well in some time," said Albret, helping himself to a roasted poultry leg. "It was my good fortune that the captain ordered me to come here—not knowing, of course, that he was sending me to the hearth of good friends. I humbly thank you for your kind hospitality, signore and signora. He nodded to each of them. Abruptly he put down his food, wiped his hands, and turned to Anabella, locking his gaze on hers.

"And Anabella. . ."

She felt the color rise to her cheeks. Until now, she had been included in the conversation but not addressed directly. Though she delighted in his presence—jubilant to see him alive and well—she felt unease because of their last encounter.

"Yes, Albret?" Her mouth felt dry, and the words sounded stiff.

"Please, tell me about your life and your concerns. I'm weary of battle talk. Have you completed the plans for the ballroom?"

She relaxed at the warmth of his question. "Yes, Albret, the plans are complete, but much work remains to be done. Mother has invited Bianca to come stay with us for a month this winter and either create a large painting or a mural for the south wall."

"That's wonderful," he exclaimed. "She will love doing it. Her talent and skills have lain idle all too long."

"Of course, with the baby. . . ," interjected Papa Antonio.

"Anabella, you will adore little Pietro," said Albret, his eyes still upon hers. "He was just learning his first steps when I left the castle."

"I'm jealous that you witnessed it and not me," said her mother, teasing. "We've not seen Baby Pietro since we were in Terni for his birth."

The conversation continued in this domestic vein. Servants cleared the table and brought sliced apples and raisins, followed by *caffe latte*. An observer would have easily concluded that the young couple was solidly betrothed. Indeed, Anabella herself nearly forgot that was not the case, so easily did the conversation flow. *How I treasure talking with Albret!* she thought. *He has always cared about what I think and do—as I for him. Unlike Frederico.*

ᴁ

Albret's visit passed all too swiftly. Much of his time was taken up with the measuring, fitting, and trying on of the special outfit he was to wear before the king's emissaries. Also, Papa Antonio kept him behind the closed door of his study, instructing him in diplomacy and protocol.

Finally, on his last night at the Turati villa, Albret sought out Anabella and asked her to stroll with him in the gardens. They had enjoyed several brief conversations and shared meals with her parents, but this would be the first opportunity of length to share time alone together.

He took her hand in the moonlight as they meandered side by side down a graveled path that circled the central fountain. Her white wool cape reflected the natural light as did his loose peasant shirt, covered only by a sleeveless rawhide vest. In the coolness of the evening, Anabella felt warmth and excitement being so close to Albret.

"Anabella," he said stopping and taking both her hands, "I wish to confide in you the perils I face in Madrid. Philip III is nothing like his strong, decisive father. The kingdom is in near ruin because of his ineptness. He has placed heavy taxes on the working people, but under such burdens, they cannot prosper. Even his advisors are urging him to give some relief to the peasants."

"So that should favor your cause."

"Yes, but the man is also stubborn and indecisive. I have heard that if he detects a threat to his power, he becomes enraged. If he resents my plea, I could be thrown in prison."

"Oh, Albret, I could not bear that."

She threw her arms about him, and he embraced her tenderly. His warm lips pressed against hers and lingered. Never before had she felt so fully part of this man she loved. Never before had she felt so in danger of losing him.

"I only tell you this, my love, in case these are our last moments together. I do not fear what lies ahead for myself, but I want you to be prepared for whatever outcome may result." He kissed her lightly on the forehead, and she laid her head against his chest.

"And our betrothal, Albert?" She dared to mention the word that had left her in such turmoil. She looked up at him hopefully, searching his face in the moonlight for the reversal she longed for.

Albret stepped back and placed his hands on her shoulders. "Anabella, I do not know who I am. I struggle within my own soul. Whether I succeed or fail in this venture—"

"But Albret, your success does not depend so much on you as on the whims of an inept ruler. *I* know who you are, and I love that identity with all my heart."

"Do you, Anabella?" He took her hand, and they strolled on down the path. "I believe you, Anabella, and that means a great deal to me. But. . ."

"That is not enough?"

"I don't know."

"God will be with you," she said, squeezing his hand. "I have prayed for that."

"You are a wonderful woman, Anabella. I admire your faith.

I treasure your loyalty and your belief in me. But until I can solve my inner conflict, I cannot honorably continue with our plans to betroth."

"Not yet?" Fear of the unknown gripped her heart.

"No, Anabella, not yet."

ða

After Albret left with Captain Gaza for Madrid, Anabella threw herself wholeheartedly into her work with the children, which she fully enjoyed. After one or two years of nurturing, Papa Antonio intended to place the children in good homes where they might serve as grooms, cooks, or house servants. Some would be apprenticed in trades as he himself had been as a child. So far, none had left the villa, but Anabella knew the time to part with her charges was fast approaching.

Albret would be gone for approximately eight weeks, which gave her a great deal of time to think about him. Although he promised to write after his meeting at the court, she felt abandoned and unsure in their relationship. *How can he profess his love and at the same time tell me I am free to see another?*

She neglected to mention a certain nobleman who had come into her life. After all, Frederico had not contacted her since the evening at the opera. In her loneliness, she recalled the *conte's* parting words—that he would call on her soon. But he had not done so.

One afternoon as she was kneading bread with the three girls in the family's care, a messenger arrived from the Soderini household with a casual invitation for her to spend the afternoon with her friends, Cecilia and Simonetta. After washing flour from her hands, she left the bread-making supervision to the head chef in the kitchen.

She found her mother helping little Gian with his letters. "Mother, a coachman is waiting to take me to the Soderini household for a visit with the sisters. Our chef has agreed to finish supervising the girls in making bread. It would please me greatly. . . ."

Her mother looked up from her task and smiled. "Yes, Anabella, that would be good for you. You've seemed sad of late. A bit of social activity will do you good. And take Luisa with you; she already knows how to make bread."

❧

Anabella and the two sisters sat at a small round table in the antechamber next to the young women's bedroom. Luisa stood behind her mistress's chair. Sections of white crocheted pieces lay on the side of the table. A maid brought a tray of tea and biscuits and then invited Luisa to pass the time in the kitchen with her.

A large window let in an abundance of light for embroidery and other handwork. Cecilia poured tea into three cups and said, "We are so happy you could come this afternoon, Anabella. I'm bursting with news."

"She talks of nothing else," said Simonetta with a sigh. "She's running out of people who are willing to listen."

"You, dear sister, are only jealous," Cecilia said with a smirk. "But your time will come, as will Anabella's."

With a satin gown the color of peaches hanging on a rack and the crocheted sections on the table, Anabella easily guessed that Cecilia had become betrothed to the Barone di Bicci. However, she waited for her friend to make the announcement.

"Everything has happened with such speed!" Cecilia said, nervously finishing her tea in a single gulp and pouring herself another. "But I am now officially betrothed to the Barone di Bicci." She paused to enjoy whatever accolades her friend might offer.

"That's fabulous, Cecilia! I am so happy for you," Anabella exclaimed with all the emotion she could muster. "I know that is what you wanted. And he seems a most worthy gentleman."

"Thank you." She smiled graciously and continued. "When my father increased the amount of my dowry—rather substantially, I might say—his father was quick to agree. They drew up the impalmare that very night! And just a week later we were betrothed at the doors of the duomo, the Santa Maria del Fiore, no less."

"That was unusually quick," said Anabella, showing the expected surprise. "And impressive to take place in front of the doors of the duomo."

"The wedding will he held there also, in one of the chapels," Cecilia said triumphantly.

"And when will that ceremony take place? Two or three years?"

"Oh, no, much sooner, probably before summer. We haven't chosen the exact date." She picked up an unfinished section of crocheting and began to ply the hook. "But as you can see, I am making my wedding apparel. This *mantilla* will drape my head. He's thirty-two-years old, so he already has his own villa completely furnished. We could move in tomorrow. He's known me since the day I was born. Our families have always been close."

Simonetta, weary of her sister's chatter, turned to Anabella. "Has Conte Bargerino ever called on you? He seemed to have eyes only for you at the Strozzi ball."

"He would be an incredible prize, Anabella, if you could catch his eye." Cecilia raised her eyebrows as though asking a question. "Much worthier of you than that commoner. . ."

"Albret Maseo," Anabella said defensively. "He is of noble character."

"But not of noble means, my dear," said Cecilia with a sarcastic laugh. "So you've not heard from the conte?"

"Actually, I have. He accompanied me to the opera *Dafne*." Anabella felt her words sounded arrogant—as if Cecilia were speaking them.

"Not at the Corsi Palace?"

Anabella nodded.

"You have risen in the world," said Simonetta. "I'm surprised even Conte Bargerino would receive such a prestigious invitation."

"There is a rumor going about that the conte may become a member of King Philip's court, one of his grandees." Cecilia smiled smugly, savoring the occasion to share inside gossip. "Would that not be a plum if you were to end up married to a gentleman of the court?"

"Perhaps you could invite your poor Italian friends for a visit." Simonetta winked in jest at her sister.

"Perhaps," said Anabella, playing their imaginative game. But, in truth, living at court had no place in dreams of her future.

≈

Upon her return that evening, Anabella found a letter, sealed and unopened on her dressing table. Carefully, she broke the seal and sat upon her bed. She recognized instantly Albret's handwriting, a neat and formal script. She took a deep breath and read the one-page message:

My dearest Anabella,

We met for three days with Francisco Gómez de Sandoval y Rojas, Duke of Lerma. All powers of state rest with him since the young king, timid and incapable of governing, concurs in his every decision. Both men live in opulence and decadence, but the Duke of Lerma revels in the art of politics. For him it appears to be a giant game of chess, in which he will use any means necessary to bring advantage to himself and the court. Amidst extravagant dinners and entertainment of every sort, we discussed the plight of the peasants.

The conte *made a lavish appearance with a large entourage, publicly fawning over the Duke of Lerma but in private making his case for throwing the peasants off his land.*

Captain Gaza praised me for my presentations, but I cannot feel optimistic about Lerma's final decision. He did appear somewhat persuaded by my argument that such heavy taxes produce diminishing returns. At least I am not in prison! Captain Gaza and the conte *did sign a truce that is to hold until we meet with an emissary in Pisa the week following Christmas. My future—our future—hangs on Lerma's decision delivered by the emissary.*

If agreeable with the Turatis, perhaps we can spend the time of Holy Nativity together, as I will be on my way to nearby Pisa. Bear with me a while longer, my love. You are always in my heart.

Albret

Anabella folded the letter and placed it in a box on her dressing table. *So love must wait until all else is settled, until Albret knows who he is and what his future holds. But dear Albret, I know who I am and who you are, and I believe it is God who holds the future.* Confused and impatient, she made her way to the family chapel.

nine

By mid-December Albret had returned to the Biliverti castle in Terni where the marchese and Bianca eagerly welcomed him. The morning after his arrival, he and the marchese toured the seigniory on horseback, making inspections of the livestock. Albret had reported his adventures in Madrid the evening before.

The rising sun lessened the chill of early morning, and a smell of dry leaves hung in the air. They rode past the yellowing grapevines and paused to discuss the crops. "The young vineyards should begin producing next year, and the older fields put forth an abundant harvest this fall," said the marchese. "As usual, your supervision of the workers brought maximum results."

"Thank you, Marchese," said Albret humbly. "You have always treated me with the utmost kindness, but now that you are home from your studies in Padua and keeping your own ledgers, perhaps you no longer need my services here."

The marchese looked surprised and flicked the reins of his horse. They rode slowly on a few minutes before he answered. "You mean because you are not betrothed to my sister?"

"If you wish to put it that way."

"I still believe you made an error in judgment, but surely you know, Albret, that you are indispensable to the seigniory. My father always depended on an overseer such as you. For the time being, at least, I am asking you to stay with me. Unless, of course, you have other interests."

"Certainly, if you need me, Marchese, I am delighted to again take up my overseeing duties now that the fighting has stopped."

The two men rode on in silence, drinking in the beauty of

the vast land of hills and valleys, flocks of sheep, herds of cattle, and fallow fields. After a time, the marchese said, "Albret, have you ever considered obtaining a university education?"

Though the question surprised him, it was not a new idea. He smiled and replied, "Marchese, I do not know what my future holds. The king may still have me arrested for taking a lead in the peasants' uprising. But in truth, my greatest interest lies with the study of law and with the new scientific discoveries. I would like to defend the scientists against false charges by the authorities."

"Such as Galileo?"

"Yes, you have spoken so highly of your university professor."

"The great man is presently in Rome, lecturing on the significance of sunspots, which may, indeed, earn him another prison term." The marchese shook his head at that sad thought, then brightly said, "Why don't you begin training a replacement for yourself and plan to enroll in the University of Padua next fall?"

"You know I do not have the means, Marchese." A shadow passed across the young man's face as he recalled another difficulty that loomed in the back of his mind. The challenge of a duel of honor. Conte Bargerino had shown him no respect in Madrid and had spoken to him directly only once: *Regardless of the outcome, we still have a score to settle.*

❧

Just before noon, the marchese and Albret rode side by side back to the castle. As they headed toward the stables, Albret noticed a group of five men on horseback ascending the private road that led up to the castle. "It appears we have visitors," he said, pointing in their direction.

"Let's intercept them," said the marchese. "I'm not expecting anyone. Let us hope they come in goodwill."

As they approached, Albret observed that the men were dressed in aristocratic attire, all with dress swords dangling at their sides. He immediately slowed his steed to drop a discrete distance behind the marchese, assuming this a matter for his master.

"Greetings and welcome to my seigniory, gentlemen. I am the Marchese Biliverti. In what way may I be of service to you?" He tipped his velvet hat but remained on horseback.

"Greetings and peace to you, Marchese," the man in the fore said with a heavy Spanish accent. He likewise tipped his hat. "I am Signore Guillermo Vasco of Siena. I come on behalf of the Conte Frederico Bargerino and seek to speak with a relative of yours, a certain Signore Albret Maseo."

Albret blanched, realizing the probable purpose of the visit.

The marchese attempted to stall, discerning the encounter to be an unfriendly one. "I have no relative by that name—"

"But I am indeed Albret Maseo, overseer of this vast seigniory." Albret urged his horse forward. "I am not of noble blood as you imagine, signore, but I am the person with whom you wish to speak." Then turning to the marchese, he said, "This is uniquely my affair, Marchese. You may leave the situation to me."

The marchese made no effort to depart.

"Please, in all due respect, Marchese, this concerns me alone."

"As you wish, Signore Maseo," said the marchese, slowly turning his horse and riding back toward the stables.

"We encountered you in Madrid, I believe. You were the spokesman for the peasants, were you not?" The man spit out the word *peasants* as if it were a curse word.

"The same," said Albret.

"But the dress, the manners, your fine speaking. . .in Madrid before the Duke of Lerma. . .we all assumed. . .the conte assumed. You are not of noble blood?"

"Only of noble character," said Albret. He recalled that Anabella had told him that on one occasion. He straightened in his saddle with the full intention of appearing arrogant. "So you come on behalf of Conte Bargerino. And what is his message?"

Signore Vasco turned to the other men and conferred in

whispers. Albret waited. At this point he became aware of his vulnerability as he sat unarmed before five men with swords.

When his companions nodded to some agreement, Signore Vasco turned back to Albret. "Conte Bargerino wishes me to convey to you his challenge to a duel of honor, signore, for an insult you flung at him in battle, calling him a coward—which he is not," he stated in a loud and daunting voice. "Do you accept or reject the challenge?"

This was precisely the message Albret had expected. And there was only one possible answer. Rejecting would label himself a coward for the rest of his life. "You may tell the conte, signore, that Signore Maseo accepts his challenge without reservation."

"Then so be it," said Signore Vasco. "All will proceed according to the *Code Duello*. I myself will serve as the conte's second. Choose a second for yourself and send him to meet me at the main crossroads in Terni, one month hence, 15 January, at noon. Your second will negotiate on your behalf the time, venue, and the measure of a win—to the death or to the first drawing of blood. As the challenged, you retain the right to choose the weapons."

"Rapiers, of course," said Albret.

"Rapiers it is, signore. You and I will not meet again until on the field of honor. Good day."

❧

Bianca sat at her easel in her studio, putting the final touches on a portrait of a client. She had asked that Albret be present while the man posed for the painting and to keep a watch on little Pietro. Now that the client had left, Albret sat in his chair holding the child on his knee.

"Do commissions still come your way, Bianca?" Pietro squirmed from his lap and toddled toward his mother.

"Very few of the sort I prefer—large biblical narratives for churches and private chapels," the artist said. "But I don't complain, for I relish time with this precious child. There is never a dearth of portrait seekers, however."

When the child picked up a broken piece of charcoal on the floor, Bianca placed a scrap of parchment before him. "I'm hoping he will have artistic tendencies," she said.

In response, Pietro looked up at his mother and promptly pushed the charcoal in his mouth. "No, no. That is not what we do with it," said Albret, retrieving the object. "I believe he is not quite ready." They both laughed, enjoying the moment. Albret cherished such domestic scenes, welcome relief from conflicts both internal and external.

"Did you know, Albret, that Mother and Father Antonio have invited us to spend a month or more with them in Florence during the Christmas season? They wish me to create a painting for their ballroom. That would be a commission."

"A fine opportunity. But no, Bianca, I did not know of your planned visit. I will be passing through Florence during that time to meet with the king's emissary in Pisa. That is when I will learn of the king's decision concerning the peasants' grievances. I feel it could go either for or against their cause."

"Marco and I would be delighted for you to go with us, and I am sure the Turatis—"

The marchese appeared in the doorway. "Albret, I wish to see you in my study." His voice sounded stern.

"Yes, of course, Marchese," Albret said and rose to go with him. "We will talk further, Bianca." The child tried to follow after him, but his mother scooped him up and brought him back.

In the study, Albret bowed slightly. "Marchese, I have every intention of telling you all that those men said to me. But at the noon meal, I didn't wish to speak in front of Bianca and the servants. And afterward. . ."

"Of course, Albret. I also wish to speak in private and hold no grievance about your timing. I watched your meeting from the stables with armed servants at the ready in case the men became hostile."

"For that I humbly thank you, Marchese."

"The scene had all the markings of a challenge to a duel. Could that be the case, Albret?" The marchese came directly to the point.

"Yes, Marchese. It comes from Conte Bargerino, against whom I clashed swords in one of the battles. As you know, he was the one who wounded me."

"And you declined his challenge, I trust?"

"No, Marchese. I felt it would dishonor my name."

"That perturbs me. But before expressing my views, I will listen to your report. Proceed."

Albret felt somewhat intimidated by the change in the marchese's manner, so amiable that morning. The two men stood facing each other. The marchese crossed his arms, and Albret clasped his hands behind him, head down, as if confessing to a parent. He recounted everything, beginning with his sword fight with the conte in battle and finishing with Signore Vasco's, "Good day."

The marchese sighed heavily. "Do you realize, Albret, that by accepting this duel of honor, you put both the Biliverti and the Bargerino families at risk? A feud could develop, placing my wife and child in danger. We were on the opposite side from the Bargerinos in the peasant uprising, though only you and a handful of servants participated. I don't know how extensively the Bargerinos of Terni were involved." The marchese paced about the room, pounding his fist into his other hand, then sat down at his desk. "Please, be seated, Albret. There is much to consider."

Albret took a chair facing the marchese. "I will have my second make it clear, Marchese, when they draw up the rules of our engagement, that the duel is only between the two of us, Conte Bargerino and myself, and that the outcome is final. He believes I insulted him by calling him a coward, which, in truth, he is."

"Let us hope that is sufficient. You know, Albret, that insulting him was a foolish thing to do."

"Yes, Marchese, I realize that. But now that I have been challenged, I must fight to defend my honor. A man's honor must be preserved at all cost. I feel passionate about honor, a defining virtue in a man's identity. Would you yourself not have accepted such a challenge?"

"Frankly, no, I would not have." The marchese folded his hands and softened his tone. "Duels are illegal in Italy at this time."

"Yes, of course, I know dueling has been banned. But that has, in no way, slowed the number of private grievances settled by the sword. Marchese, you can easily refuse such challenges. Your reputation is firm. You are revered in the community. You are powerful and of noble blood."

"Society is changing, Albret. There are deposed nobles begging in the streets of Rome, and at the same time, common men have risen to great wealth and prestige. Regard Antonio Turati, who married my mother, the widow of a Biliverti."

"But he is a barone—"

"A purchased title. But that is of little consequence."

"Marchese, I doubt that you know how my father died." Albret felt his hands begin to quiver as he recalled an event that had so totally affected his life.

"No, I only know that you were a small child when your widowed mother came to work for Bianca's family in Rome. Please, enlighten me." The marchese leaned back in his chair and folded his arms across his chest.

"Mother tells me that Father was a young, prosperous silk merchant. On several occasions, a particular client had tried to cheat him in trade. I'm not sure of the particulars, but when my father finally brought it to his attention, he became enraged and accused him of besmirching his good name. He challenged him to a duel. My father refused, even though he was quite adept with the sword. Only days later, my father was ambushed while traveling and murdered."

"I did not know, Albret. I am sorry."

"My mother was unable either to run the business or turn a profit by selling it. It seems this client had spread false rumors about my father's business practices and let it be known that my father had dishonored his name by refusing the challenge. No one would pay a fair price for the business, and thus we were reduced to poverty."

"I see. So in a way this is avenging your father?"

"Perhaps."

The marchese rose and removed a framed scripture verse from the wall. The words were embroidered with scarlet thread on canvas. "Anabella made this for me several years ago. By what I'm about to say, I place myself in the role of a father—or at least older brother—but I think there is a message here for you." He laid the object on his desk in front of Albret.

Anabella?

"It's taken from Proverbs 15:33. Why don't you read it aloud?"

Albret read, " 'The fear of the Lord is the instruction of wisdom; and before honour is humility.' " Obviously, the marchese was chastising him for his decision, putting him further on the defensive.

"I do not approve of this duel, Albret, but I do understand your position. In the end, it is your decision—your honor to consider. I only wish to point out that you must go to the Lord to find wisdom for your decision, and I ask you to remember that the path to honor is humility."

They both stood, and he shook Albret's hand. "Think on these words."

ten

The marchese, Bianca, and little Pietro arrived at the Turati villa with their entourage of servants, including Albret's mother, Sylvia, three days before Christmas. Anabella had not been so happy in weeks. With no further word from Albret and no contact from Conte Bargerino since the evening at the opera, she had felt sad and abandoned by both men. Now with the house filled with laughter and the sharing of stories, her spirits lifted. She and her mother vied for the privilege of caring for little Pietro.

That morning the family gathered in the ballroom to discuss the artwork Bianca had come to do.

"Would you not prefer to paint on canvas rather than do a mural, Bianca?" said Marco. "I could build you a double easel."

"Yes, that would be easier for me to maneuver," said Bianca.

They all agreed to a framed painting as they stood lined up in front of the empty expanse of the designated wall.

"We've all been thinking of a biblical narrative," said Papa Antonio. He scratched his bearded chin and stared at the space as if imagining various possibilities.

"What would you think of an event from the Old Testament?" asked Anabella's mother. "Something that tells a story and has a message."

"And I suggest a marble statue on either side of the painting," said Anabella.

"Now we are really increasing the cost," said her ever frugal stepfather.

"But Father Antonio, I know several very talented sculptors—lesser-known ones," said Bianca with enthusiasm.

"I like Anabella's idea, and the sculptures could reflect the biblical figures."

Pietro squirmed down from his mother's arms and ran to the wall. He raised his hands and leaned his back against it, grinning mischievously at the adults.

"Look at that," said Anabella. "We must have children in the painting. Pietro could be a model."

Bianca laughed. "If only I could get him to sit still long enough to pose! But that is a wonderful idea. What would you think if I portrayed Jacob and his two wives and twelve sons?"

"You'll have to leave out either Rachel or Benjamin," pointed out Marco.

"Yes, of course, she died giving her second son life," said Bianca. "But what do you think? We could have their dwellings and extended families here on the right. Then Joseph could be on his way to check on his brothers who are tending their flocks on this side. That would allow for a grand landscape between the two centers of interest."

"Models would be easy to find," said Anabella. "Mother and Papa Antonio could pose as Jacob and Leah."

Her mother frowned.

"Of course, Bianca would have to make your eyes look weak. . ." Anabella grimaced at the thought.

"I like that idea very much," said Marco. "Albret will be here in the next day or so. Some work details prevented him from coming with us. I imagine him as the young Joseph, clean-shaven and strong."

Albret? He had said he might come in his letter, which she had shared with her parents, but as usual, no one had mentioned that he would be here.

Thus they all agreed on the painting and retired to the salon to discuss the details. Bianca seemed eager to begin, and Marco offered to go into Florence to purchase the canvas, a wooden frame to stretch it across, and lumber for building two oversized easels.

Suddenly Giorgio appeared at the door to announce, "Signore Albret Maseo has arrived and awaits in the entrance." Anabella felt her heart stop then beat rapidly.

"Shall we then go greet 'Joseph'?" asked Papa Antonio, naming him in jest after his proposed modeling role. The group rushed to the entry hall, Anabella lagging behind. The last time she had seen him, Albret had suggested those moments might be their last together. Fortunately, he had not been thrown in prison, and here he was, accompanied by Massetti as his attendant.

After greeting each of the others with great fanfare, he approached Anabella and took her hands in his. "Anabella, I am so delighted to see you."

Her lips parted to respond, but alas, words stuck in her throat.

Marco rescued the awkward moment by relating the family agreement on the painting Bianca was to do. "And we have chosen you to model as Joseph on his way to check on his brothers."

Albret laughed at the idea but appeared pleased nonetheless. "I like the subject matter," he said. "And Jacob's two families would represent what? Duty and love?"

"Brilliant!" exclaimed Bianca. "Jacob married Leah out of duty and Rachel out of love."

"And the message would be duty before love?" asked Anabella's mother.

Anabella clasped her hands together, damp with perspiration in reaction to her mother's words. Surely she was unaware of the comparison to Albret's position. And did Albret see the obvious parallel? "Perhaps love first could fortify duty," she blurted out.

Albret looked at her in alarm. Had she crossed a line into the male realm of values? Clearly he had understood her meaning. "A man's honor comes with the performance of what he deems his duty," he said. With his jaw firmly set, he turned to Papa Antonio. "I wish to thank you for your hospitality. It will be a great pleasure to pass the season of Nativity with your family."

"Costanza and I are delighted that you can spend these days with us," said Papa Antonio. "And when must you travel to Pisa?"

"I am to meet with the king's emissary 29 December. If all goes well, I will return with good news on New Year's Day. If not, Massetti will bring you the news."

Luisa brought a tray of refreshments, and the group returned to the salon. Anabella felt a tenseness between herself and Albret. He chose a single chair rather than the settee he could have shared with her. Since he politely included her in the conversation, no one else seemed to notice his coolness. Apparently she had offended him with her suggestion that love need not wait.

Voices rose and fell as topics leaped from the political situation to harvests to commerce to Pietro's antics. Little Pietro made the rounds, seeking and gaining attention from each person present. When he finally snuggled up in Anabella's lap, she glanced triumphantly toward Albret, her eyes sending the message: *This little one loves me.*

Suddenly Anabella's mother suggested, "Why don't you and Albret set up the *presepio* in the chapel? The nativity pieces are stored in the armoire in the upstairs hallway."

Before Anabella could protest, Albret jumped up. "Splendid idea, signora. We would love to do just that." He took the sleepy and protesting Pietro from Anabella's arms and handed the child to Bianca.

As the two headed toward the stairs, Anabella overheard her mother say, "It's obvious he adores her. I don't understand. . ."
Nor do I, Mother, she thought.

❧

Albret knelt next to Anabella on the satin cushion before the altar as together they arranged the five-inch figurines of the presepio. Love, rather than duty, surged to the front of Albret's mind when his hand accidentally brushed Anabella's as they each placed shepherds next to the manger. The scent of rose water wafted from her long dark hair, which was pulled back with a scarlet ribbon. Her earlier mention of love had set ablaze the passion he kept buried deep in his heart. *Ah, Anabella is so strong. I love her even more for her patience.*

"We hope each year to expand the set with more pieces," said Anabella, "since the family set remained with Marco in Terni."

He reached into the box that lay between them and withdrew another piece. Unwrapping it, he discovered it was the Baby Jesus and started to place the piece in the manger.

"Oh, no, that must wait until Christmas morning," said Anabella, looking up into his eyes. "Not yet can we put *Santo Bambino* in his place." Her voice was soft and tender.

Anabella, my love, let's be betrothed today and marry tomorrow! Such thoughts ran wildly through his head until he reminded himself of the two hurdles he first must leap: *Not only do I need to find favor with the king, but also I have my honor to defend in a duel. Be patient, my heart!*

He gently rewrapped the figurine and returned it to the box. "And where do you place the magi?" he asked, looking about for a proper place.

"I'll show you," she said as together they unwrapped the three pieces. "Here at the end of the altar rail." She took one of the kings, and he followed her with the others. "They begin their journey here," she said. They lined up the kings bearing gifts.

"So, you think they can journey all the way to Bethlehem by 6 January?" *By then I will know what message the king's emissary brings me in Pisa.*

"They made it last year," she said with a laugh. "If not, we will hurry them along. They must get their gifts to the Christ child for Epiphany."

Albret savored the sound of her laugh. It reminded him of tinkling bells. He wanted to scoop her up in his arms, bury his head in her ruffled collar, and then smother her with ardent kisses. But instead, he said, "Let's go into the city and see if the shepherds have come down from the hills to play bagpipes. We have no *zampognari* who live near Terni, but I remember them from my childhood in Rome at Christmastime."

"Indeed, we have zampognari who live high in the mountains. They perform every day in Florence and stay in town right up to Christmas Eve," she said, pleasure shining in her eyes. "They wear shaggy sheepskin vests and leather breeches tied at the knees and white stockings. We can take Luisa and Giorgio with us. They will find it delightful."

❧

The day before Christmas dawned bright and unseasonably warm. The Turatis had dismissed all the servants for the holiday except the orphan children. Bianca, of course, retained Signora Sylvia Maseo, Albret's mother, to help her with Pietro. Anabella and the other women, as well as Papa Antonio, were all involved in the preparation of food—especially for such a grand occasion. Thus they had spent the morning selecting the very best of fresh products at the markets and the afternoon preparing the celebratory meal to be eaten later that day.

In the evening, Anabella, along with family and guests, gathered on the western terrace, framed by a stone balustrade. Although Albret had spent much of the past three days at Anabella's side, he seemed distracted—even when they had gone to hear the shepherds play their bagpipes. He now stood beside her watching the sun slowly set over the city of Florence. The silhouette of the duomo's huge dome stood out above everything else. As the sun dropped from the rose-colored sky, a distant cannon blast broke the stillness, signaling the advent of Christmas.

"*Buon Natale!*" said Albret, placing his hand at the back of Anabella's waist and brushing a kiss across her lips. He then quickly withdrew his hand.

"Buon Natale, Albret," she whispered. *Buon Natale, wherever you are!* Indeed, his mind seemed to have taken him far from her side.

The Christmas greeting was passed from person to person before the group returned inside to partake of the sumptuous meal. In keeping with Italian tradition, they had fasted for the past twenty-four hours and were well ready to devour the meatless meal of *capitone*—a large eel—and *baccalà*—codfish—deep-fried vegetables, crusty loaves of bread, and pasta of various shapes and sizes.

Afterward, they traveled in three carriages, to make room for the children and servants, to the duomo for midnight mass. Again Albret was beside Anabella as they moved with the crowd past the grand presepio displayed at the front of the cathedral. Here, not only were the holy family, the shepherds, and wise men represented, but also an elaborate array of miniature personages and animals formed a fantastic panorama.

"These figures in the marketplace look so real, right down to the warts and wrinkles," said Anabella with enthusiasm.

"And this peasant family around the table," said Albret pointing. "The food appears real enough to eat. And look at the little dog snapping up the scraps thrown under the table."

"The fine carriages and horses, the musicians, the shoemaker, the blacksmith."

Church bells announced the service was about to begin. Albret took her hand, and they found their way to places next to his mother, Signora Maseo, and the rest of the family. Anabella relished the singing of carols, the prayers, the liturgy, the chants, and the bishop's homily. Once amid her joy, she glanced toward Albret. His face seemed drawn and pensive.

It was nearly two of the clock in the morning when the carriages pulled up to the villa. Bianca and Marco rushed directly to their quarters to put to bed the sleeping Pietro. Papa Antonio whisked his wife off to the kitchen, where he would brew his cherished caffe latte.

Albret and Anabella stood awkwardly at the bottom of the staircase. Light from a large candle on a stand flickered across Albret's face. He took her hands. "You look lovely tonight."

He stumbled over the words.

"I'm surprised you noticed me at all," she said, a frown on her brow. "You seemed to have left me after we enjoyed the presepio together. I don't want to sound peevish, but frankly, Albret, I feel you are pulling me to you with one hand and pushing me away with the other."

He dropped her hands and clasped his own. Looking down, he shuffled his feet and finally answered, "Anabella, I thank you for your patience. Since I have no claim, you are free."

"That is no answer at all. You are only enforcing this. . .this ambivalence. I am tiring of it, Albret." Her voice, though void of anger, carried a strong and honest message.

"I am sorry, Anabella."

She turned to go up the stairs, but he clutched her wrist. "I did notice you tonight, Anabella. Not just your beauty. I watched you during the service—your faith is so real, so strong. I pray for God's direction and guidance, but He seems distant to me. You *know* He is with you."

"I do, Albret." Her voice softened. "Are you concerned about your meeting in Pisa?"

"It's possible to win the war but lose what we fought for— more rights for the peasants. Yes, so much depends on whether I was able to convince the Duke of Lerma and thus the king."

"I will pray for a good outcome. And peace for you, Albret."

"Please do." He clasped both her hands tightly and smiled. He then took a candle from a shelf beside the staircase, placed it in a holder, and lit it from the large candle on the stand. He handed it to her. "Buon Natale."

"Buon Natale, Albret." She started up the stairs with the candle.

"And don't forget to place *Santo Bambino* in his manger," he whispered after her.

She turned and smiled in spite of her frustration, then blew him a kiss.

eleven

Anabella as well as the rest of the household slept until nearly noon on Christmas Day. After a light meal topped with *panettone*—a light yeast cake made with candied fruit—and *strufoli*—little balls of dough fried in oil and dipped in honey—the family made their way to the chapel.

The orphan children were delighted to find that the Santo Bambino had "magically appeared" in his manger. Gian, the youngest, was chosen to move the wise men a short distance down the altar rail. He blushed with excitement as he solemnly performed his role. Everyone stood at the front of the chapel watching, and they clapped when the figures were in place.

"There will be gifts for each of you on 6 January when the wise men make it to the manger," said Anabella's mother.

"For most of them, this is their first Christmas celebration," explained Papa Antonio, directing his words to Marco and Bianca.

"You and mother and 'Bella have made wonderful contributions to these children's lives," said Marco. "I commend you for your efforts."

"It has been as much our pleasure as theirs," said Anabella. "I will miss them when they leave." She looked over the little group of children and noticed Luisa and Giorgio standing very close together, possibly holding hands. She reached over and slipped her hand in Albret's. He pressed it gently and did not release it until all sat down.

"I think I have found work for most of them except for Gian, who is not yet ready," said Papa Antonio. "Costanza and I will take them to their new homes day after the morrow. Giorgio and Luisa will both serve in the Soderini household, so we will continue to see them from time to time."

Papa Antonio invited everyone to be seated. He read the Christmas story from Luke 2 in the family Bible and offered a long prayer that included everyone by name. He asked comfort and guidance for Albret in his upcoming meeting in Pisa.

The rest of the day, traditionally a time for families and relatives, passed with the men playing chess and the women engaging in various games with the children. Anabella never found herself alone with Albret.

ଛ

The day following Christmas, the Turatis received several guests in keeping with the custom of visiting with friends on that day. The Soderini family arrived in mid-afternoon just as Papa Antonio's business partner, Paolo, was leaving.

In the entry hall, Paolo turned to Albret and said, "I understand you made a splendid argument before the Duke of Lerma in Madrid. My congratulations, young man." He vigorously shook Albret's hand. "But if the outcome does not go well in Pisa, you have me to blame for getting you into this, for indeed, it was I who recommended you to represent Captain Gaza on the advice of Signore Turati."

Anabella noticed that Papa Antonio cringed at this revelation, but still he concurred. "Yes, we sent a message along with the cannon bearers that you would be an asset to the negotiations." He lowered his voice and added, "But we must keep our involvement in the strictest secrecy."

"I understand," said Albret. "But I thank you both for the confidence you have placed in me. I hope the result will prove I have served my countrymen well."

"Ah, here comes the Soderini family. You must tarry a moment to meet them, Paolo," said Papa Antonio.

After Paolo's departure and introductions between the Soderinis and the Bilivertis, the two families gathered in the salon. Sylvia took Bianca's baby, Pietro, upstairs for a nap. Luisa arrived with a tray of *pinocchiati*, delicate pine-nut sweets, and spicy *panforte*, made with fruit and nuts. Another girl brought a container of coffee with cups and saucers.

The men and women divided automatically and went to separate sides of the large room.

"Wasn't the presepio at the duomo just magnificent?" asked Cecilia as she took a chair next to Anabella.

"We saw you at the church but couldn't get through the crowds to speak," said Simonetta.

"Yes, it was exquisite," agreed Anabella. Her mother and Bianca nodded agreement. "The children in our care were wide-eyed with excitement."

The conversation continued thus until Anabella changed the topic and explained the painting Bianca would do for the ballroom. The sisters seemed duly impressed and nodded politely.

After a pause, Cecilia spoke with much enthusiasm, "All of you are coming to the New Year's ball at the Uffizi Palace, are you not? I'm sure you have received invitations from the Duke of Tuscany. The marchese and marchesa would, of course, be welcome as your guests."

"That would be grand," said Bianca, "but Marco is returning to Terni in the morning. He is not comfortable away from the seigniory for an extended time. And, of course, as a married woman, I would not attend without him."

"And Albret departs in the morning also," said Anabella.

"Back to Terni?" asked Simonetta.

"In truth, he has an important mission in Pisa." Anabella did not wish to reveal his purpose, for she surmised the Soderinis had not been on the side of the peasants. As all the nobility knew, it could be dangerous to reveal one's political views.

"Then why don't you come with us?" encouraged Cecilia, returning to her enthusiasm.

"Come where, my dears?" asked Signora Soderini. She and Anabella's mother had been deep in conversation over the contents of the confectioneries.

"The New Year's ball at the Uffizi, Mother," said Simonetta.

"We had not planned to attend," said Anabella's mother. "We are busy placing our protégés in new employment. This is the time of year both businesses and families make decisions."

"But Anabella could come with us," proposed Cecilia.

"Yes, our coachman can easily stop by for her," said Signora Soderini. "What do say, Signora Turati?"

Anabella had never been inside the Duke of Tuscany's most splendid palace. This would be a rare opportunity. She hesitated to go to such a grand affair without Albret, but his polite coolness had begun to annoy her. The pleasant image of his lighting a candle for her at the bottom of the stairs and his notice of her faith flashed across her mind. *Yet he is still ambivalent*, she decided. "I would love to go, Mother."

Her mother seemed to be weighing her decision also but finally said, "That is most kind of you, Signora. Yes, she may go, and I would like to send my attendant, Clarice, along."

After the Soderinis had departed amid a flurry of polite compliments and well wishes for the season, Anabella overheard her mother make an alarming remark to Papa Antonio: ". . .permitted her to attend the Duke's ball. Will not Conte Bargerino be in Pisa?"

"I presume so," Papa Antonio had answered.

Why would Conte Bargerino be in Pisa? And why would that have anything to do with her or the Duke's ball? No matter how much Albret annoyed her, Anabella wanted to run to him and have him fold her in his arms. For so long that had been her place of comfort. He never used to keep secrets from her. But now Albret seemed unreachable, and besides, he was engrossed in a scientific discussion with Marco. *I will just go to the ball and take my mind off all this*, she decided.

৯

Anabella rode in the lead carriage with the Soderini family, the servants following in the second vehicle. They crossed the Arno River on the *Ponte Vecchio*, the old covered bridge lined with jewelry shops, closed on New Year's Eve. Save for the outside carriage lanterns flickering light across the passengers' faces, all was dark until they emerged on the other side.

Suddenly they burst into a fantasy land of light from torches lined along the vast expanse of the Uffizi Palace. "How magnificent!" exclaimed Anabella. "And the guards in formation all in uniform."

"Listen," said Cecilia, equally delighted. "There's music, too!"

Two groomsmen approached the carriage and took the reins of the horses. A guard stepped forward and assisted the ladies in their exit. He escorted the party past marble statues by Michelangelo and Donatello to the grand entrance. From there another uniformed officer led them down a splendidly decorated hallway with enormous paintings by Leonardo da Vinci, Botticelli, and Lippi. When they arrived at the threshold of the ballroom, the officer loudly announced their arrival. The Duke of Tuscany himself and his wife greeted them with handshakes and words of welcome.

Anabella tried not to gawk at the opulence—gilded tracery, ornate candelabra placed before mirrors, lighted chandeliers suspended from the vaulted ceiling, musicians playing stringed instruments, and a flurry of servant girls offering drinks and delicacies of every sort.

Cecilia's betrothed, the Barone di Bicci, and Simonetta's friend, the Visconte Strozzi, approached them almost immediately. The visconte caught the attention of a girl with a tray of goblets and handed one to each in the group.

Following polite greetings and inquiries into everyone's state of health, the barone turned to Anabella. "The Conte Bargerino is here and has been asking if anyone has seen you. Of course, he needs some cheering up after all he has been through." The barone rolled his eyes, and the Soderini sisters smiled knowingly.

"And, Romolo, just what has the conte been through?" asked Anabella, not wishing to be left unaware. The surprised look on the barone's face told her he had assumed she *knew*.

"Ah, here comes the conte now!"

After a brief conversation, the group broke into couples, and their personal attendants, including Clarice, faded into the wood paneling to watch their charges from afar.

Conte Frederico Bargerino took Anabella's goblet and set it beside his on a small, marble-top table between two freestanding candelabra. With his hand behind her waist, he waltzed her onto the dance floor. "The emerald green dress becomes you, my dear. I hoped you would be here tonight, but I am surprised," he whispered in her ear.

With her hair up and secured by jade combs, Anabella felt elegant dancing with the handsome and dashing conte. She smiled up at him. "Why would you be surprised, Frederico? My stepfather has known the Duke of Tuscany for some time."

"No, no, my dear," he said with a laugh. "Of course you would receive an invitation. I mean. . .are the Barone Turati and your mother here tonight? You seemed to be with the Soderinis."

"I did come with the Soderinis," Anabella said, recalling her mother's remark to Papa Antonio that Frederico would likely be in Pisa. "My parents were involved with other concerns today and declined the invitation." She felt emboldened to probe further, for his interest in her seemed quite apparent. "You are surprised to see me here tonight, but Frederico, I am surprised I haven't heard from you since the opera."

Suddenly his demeanor became quite solemn. "Anabella, do you not know about the letter your. . .Barone Turati sent to me?"

"What letter?" she asked in astonishment. The music became louder and the dance livelier. It was no longer possible to talk. But as soon as the number had finished, Frederico led her to where he had set their goblets, only to discover they had been whisked away. They sat side by side in armless brocaded chairs and were soon brought other goblets as well as a little plate of *cannoli*, crisp pastry shells filled with creamy ricotta cheese and candied fruit.

"What letter, Frederico?"

"I thought you knew, Anabella, and were probably complicit in it." He set the cannoli on a table and took her hand. "Barone Turati said that he and your mother were asking me to refrain from contacting you. He said your interest leaned toward another. Is that true, Anabella?"

"I don't understand why they would say that." She frowned trying to imagine why her mother had so suddenly reversed her opinion of the conte—or were they just defending Albret? "Yes, I will tell you truthfully, there is someone else. But we have no commitment between us."

"Then certainly there is no harm in our enjoying each other's company." His face brightened. "Your beauty is beyond compare, Anabella. Just while we have been sitting here, several of my friends have passed by, envying my good fortune. You would be a treasured asset to any man."

"Thank you, Frederico. I suppose that is a compliment." She sensed color rise to her cheeks. Somehow being an "asset" of any kind felt uncomfortable.

But for the first time, he seemed interested in listening to her. She told him about the wonderful presepio at the duomo—which he had not seen—and talked of the orphans that her family befriended. Eventually, she felt enough at ease to ask him in a teasing way, "Romolo alluded to the possibility that you may need cheering up this evening. Would that be the case, Frederico?"

Frederico laughed and said, "Romolo doesn't know what he's talking about. But sitting here with you, Anabella, cheers me sufficiently." He paused but remained lighthearted. "I have a serious threat on my life, but as a man of courage, I can face any challenge."

"Oh, Frederico! That is horrible. Who could possibly want to kill you?" Her eyes were wide with shock, and she felt a surge of sympathy for the man carrying such a grave burden.

"It's a duel of honor, and I have an excellent reputation with the sword. 'Tis the other man who lies awake in fear. Perhaps you would like to be a witness when I defend my honor."

"Honor?" she said, thinking of Albret and his need to prove himself honorably. "Why do men become obsessed with honor?"

"Oh, I don't know," he said twirling the end of his mustache. "For glory, I guess. And we like to impress the women we love. Would you be impressed if I were to win a duel?"

"Impressed? I would be horrified if you killed someone—and even more so if you were slain!"

"You would care if I were killed? That touches my heart." He laid his hand across his chest. "But let's dance."

Again they swirled out on the floor. Anabella, dazzled by her surroundings and caught up in the conte's personal revelations to her, yielded to his flattery.

"I've waited my whole life for someone like you," he whispered in her ear. "Not only are you the most beautiful woman here tonight, but you are someone with whom I can share my most intimate concerns."

"And I am so happy in your arms," Anabella said softly. Albret had been slipping away, even while they were together. This felt more comforting.

Ever the gentleman, Frederico bowed slightly at the end of the number. "Thank you for dancing with me, Anabella. You are ever so light in my arms. Let's stroll out on the terrace and take in some fresh air." With hundreds of candles burning and as many people dancing, the air had become warm and stale in the ballroom.

Anabella found Clarice and retrieved her black wool cape. The couple stepped into the crisp, cool night. The clear sky shone with diamondlike stars. Frederico took her hand, and together, they looked out over the city of Florence. Mostly it lay in darkness, but here and there light seeped from windows or a row of torches would bring a building into focus. In the distance, they could see the rounded silhouette of mountains. They talked pleasantly about the beauty that surrounded them.

Anabella felt the warmth of Frederico's arm about her

shoulders and thrilled to the romantic circumstance that engulfed her. After a period of silence, Frederico turned to her, slid his hands down her arms, and clasped her hands. Looking directly into her eyes, he said, "Anabella, I desire for you to be my wife. This moment could last a lifetime, and you could be forever happy in my arms." He kissed her lightly on the lips. "We would not need a long betrothal. Please say you will consent to become the Contessa Bargerino."

The kiss brought a flood of conflicting emotion—and unexpected desire. But the thought of marriage to this man she was only beginning to know and like came as a jolt. Not knowing how to respond, she stammered, "That is not for me to answer, Frederico. Only my brother, Marco, the Marchese Biliverti, may make such arrangements. I–I don't know." She pulled back from him and looked again out over the city.

"Then I will write a letter to him in Terni, asking if we may draw up the impalmare," he said with triumph, as if an agreement had already been made. He placed his hand possessively at her back and guided her toward the ballroom.

Just outside the doorway stood her mother's personal attendant stony-faced. She could not have been close enough to hear their conversation, but she would not have missed the kiss. Feeling guilty but making no apology, Anabella handed her wool cape to the woman. "Thank you, Clarice."

twelve

Albret spent the eve of the new year, 1613, traveling back from his critical meeting with the king's emissary in Pisa. He and his attendant, Massetti, stopped for the night in the little village of Empoli and rented a room. After settling in, they went downstairs to the local tavern and ordered a light meal of lamb stew and bread. The two men sat at the end of a long wooden table crowded with other merrymakers. The tavern became unruly and boisterous as midnight approached.

Just as the bell in the church tower pealed twelve times, Albret and Massetti tinked goblets.

"To the new year," said Massetti. "Prosperity, happiness, and God's blessings!"

"To the brave peasants of Tuscany," said Albret. "May they, too, find prosperity, happiness, and God's blessings in the coming year!"

In the room, cheers and toasts soon lowered to whispers so that all could hear the crashing noises from the village. Some in the crowd even rushed outdoors to watch as the townspeople dropped pots and pans, pottery, and metal objects from their windows. Albret recalled that in the past this tradition was meant to scare away evil spirits. But now in the modern seventeenth century, it served only as a means of welcoming the new year.

When the patrons began to disperse, Albret and Massetti were better able to hear each other.

"We could not have wished for better words from the king's emissary," said Albret as he held up his goblet to be refilled by the young girl waiting tables.

"Certainly from the part I heard, they could not have been

more welcome," agreed Massetti, motioning to the girl to refill his goblet as well. "The emissary simply read the declaration that gives the peasants the right to compensation if they must leave the conte's land or employment if they stay. Then a fairer distribution of taxes among the peasants. And what was the third?"

"Unfortunately, no reprieve on working on the roads. However, they may choose to split their month of labor contribution into two segments. That will help some," said Albret.

"And I don't dare to ask the amount of the purse, signore, that you received in commendation from King Philip." Massetti looked away in mock disinterest.

"He never stated the amount of pesos, but as you can imagine, the two heavy bags of silver coins make up a substantial amount." Albret suddenly stood up and laid some coins on the table to cover their fare. "We need to return to our room as that money lies unprotected."

Upstairs in their room, Albret immediately set a burning candle on the floor, dropped to his knees, and pulled the bags from under his bed. "They seem to weigh the same," he said with relief before putting them back. He set the candle on a stand by the bed. "One, of course, is for Captain Gaza for leading the fight, and mine is for—as the emissary termed it—the persuading argument. The irony is in the source of the purse."

"And what is the source, signore?" said Massetti, eager to hear the complete story. For a short time, Albret had met in a room alone with the emissary behind closed doors while Massetti waited outside.

"The irony is. . ." Albret sat on the edge of the bed, rubbing his hands together and weighing whether he should reveal this piece of information. Then elation over his success took over, and he said, "You are my friend, Massetti, and I know I can trust you not to reveal what I am telling you."

"You have my word on it, signore." Massetti sat down in the

room's only chair, folded his arms, and waited.

"The Duke of Lerma, that is to say in essence the king, does not like disturbances and unrest in his realm. He desires loyalty from his subjects above all else. He has no qualms about bleeding the peasants himself as long as they remain placid. What the duke detests, the emissary told me, is the use of state militia against the king's subjects, for he wishes to keep them in ready reserve for foreign conquests or defense."

"But he didn't use the state militia; it was just an uprising by the peasants against some nobles and their mercenaries—"

"Ah, but apparently our conte had requested assistance from the king and was refused." Albret removed his doublet and hung it on the bedpost, then began preparing for bed while he talked. "In Madrid, when I revealed that Conte Bargerino had instigated the rebellion himself for his own glory—in hopes of gaining the king's favor—the duke became enraged. So said the emissary. I myself had noticed little emotion in the duke, but of course, he is shrewd."

Albret sat back on the bed in his nightshirt. "And here's the irony of it all, Massetti. The emissary told me that the king levied a substantial fine on Conte Bargerino for causing the insurgency, stirring up unrest in Tuscany, and the resultant loss of life—as well as disloyalty to the throne. Also, the conte has borne a heavy cost for the war and, because he has badly managed his assets, is now reduced to a mere fraction of the wealth he inherited. The full amount of his fine lies in the two bags under this bed, in my possession!"

"That is real justice! And you, my good friend, have brought honor and glory to *your* name," said Massetti as he shook Albret's hand. He then readied himself for bed, blew out the candle, and soon was snoring.

But, Albret lay with his hands behind his head and stared into the darkness. He certainly had won. But the triumph did not seem quite as glorious as he had hoped. *Yes, now I have honor and wealth. I am worthy of Anabella's love for me.*

But alas, there is yet the duel of honor.

He rolled over and closed his eyes, but sleep evaded him. He relived the meeting with the king's emissary, often interrupted by heavy snores from his companion. The words of the Scripture embroidered by Anabella for her brother came to mind: "The fear of the Lord is the instruction of wisdom; and before honour is humility."

Albret drifted off to sleep with a simple prayer on his lips for two things he felt he was lacking—wisdom and humility.

☙

The two men arrived at the Turati villa in mid-afternoon under a gray sky. A sharp wind had come up the last hour of their travel, slowing their horses and chilling their unprotected faces. A groom met them to take their horses just as large drops of rain began to fall.

Inside, Albret warmed his hands at a fire roaring in the salon's grand fireplace. He turned as the Turatis entered and smiled amiably, as well as triumphantly, at Anabella. "Please sit here beside me, Anabella," he said, indicating a place on the settee.

He noted that his own delight failed to reflect in her face. But that was easily explained. After all, he had deliberately been reserved before his journey in an effort to protect her from false hope.

"Good afternoon, Albret," she said as she sat at the far end of the red velvet settee. Albret took his place on the other end. Massetti, as his personal attendant on this mission, stood behind him.

"We are all eager to hear about your encounter with the king's emissary in Pisa," said Signore Turati, taking a chair next to his wife.

Clarice brought in a tray of cups, saucers, and a kettle. She set them on a table at the side of the room. "Shall I pour, signora?"

"No, that will be all, Clarice," Signora Turati said. Then turning her attention to Albret, she observed, "The fact that you have returned gives us encouragement, and I can see good fortune written across your face."

Albret again was wearing the outfit especially made for his meeting with the Duke of Lerma in Madrid and looked the part of the important diplomat he was. "Indeed, I do bring back good news for the valiant peasants who fought for their rights, signore and signora. And I thank you again for the important contribution you made to our success in battle. Had we not won on the battlefield, there would never have been a resort to diplomacy. The conte's expectations of winning were not met in Madrid."

He glanced at Anabella and was pleased to notice her following his narrative with interest.

"If the conte lost, then you and the peasants must have gained," said Signore Antonio.

At that moment, Bianca came downstairs, accompanied by Albret's mother, Sylvia, who was carrying Pietro. Albret stood to greet them. He kissed his mother on both cheeks and patted the baby. "I'm just beginning to tell my news. Come in."

"Thank the good Lord you are here and looking well," said his mother. "You must have good news."

Anabella got up and poured tea. She served full cups all around, ending with Albret. Albret briefly caught her eyes looking into his. They each held opposite rims of the saucer for a brief second. *I want to tell you everything, Anabella, for our future is nearly assured.*

"I was just saying that the conte lost, and we won on all scores—save one—that we were fighting for," said Albret with exuberance. He then told of the contents of the document that he would take to Captain Gaza. He neglected to mention, however, the conte's heavy fine and how the money had been passed on to himself and the captain as rewards. He would save that for Anabella alone.

❧

"Anabella, wait!" Albret called after the family had broken

bread together the following morning. Anabella had rushed from the table as soon as everyone finished the meal. He rose and followed her. "Please, wait, Anabella. You seem to disappear every time we have an opportunity to be together."

She stopped in the open area that led to the salon. "We have spent a great deal of time together, Albret, since you arrived."

"I mean alone," he said, sounding defensive.

"I welcome you as an old family friend and enjoy your company as do my parents," she said averting her eyes. "Congratulations on your achievements—both on the battlefield and with diplomacy. There is nothing more to say." She smiled politely and turned to go.

"I have not told the whole story. I've saved some good news for your ears alone." He gently took her elbow, and she turned back toward him.

"All right. Tell me," she said.

"Could we go. . .somewhere?" He looked around helplessly. This was not going well.

"I'm working on a dress, but I could take a few minutes," she said not unpleasantly. "Let's go to the receiving room. There is a small fireplace in there, but you will need to build the fire. Giorgio and the other boys have been placed, so we are short on servants."

"Building fires is one of my jobs at the Biliverti castle," said Albret.

"I didn't mean. . ." She left the sentence hanging, but Albret knew exactly what she meant—he *was* a servant.

Though elegant, the small room was damp and cold. Rain beat against the windows, and wind howled around the corners outside. Albret knelt and adroitly placed the logs and kindling in the fireplace. "I'll be back shortly," he said, taking a metal box and tongs with him.

He returned with a burning coal from the salon fireplace, which he placed under the stacked wood. Soon the fire blazed brightly. "That will add some warmth and a bit of light on this dark morning," he said, trying to sound cheerful. He pulled a chair up next to hers in front of the fireplace—but not too close.

"I am happy for your success, Albret. And your honor," she said, looking into the fire. "What else do you have to tell me?"

When she turned and their eyes met, Albret's heart nearly leaped from his chest. She was in reach now, the woman he loved with all his heart, mind, and body. She recognized his success and his honor! There only remained his duel of honor to fight against Conte Frederico Bargerino. He wondered if she remembered the conte from that carnival ball in Terni two years ago when he had watched her dance with him. Deliberately, Albret had always referred to him simply as "the conte."

"The conte, against whom we fought, is indeed an evil man, Anabella. He incited the uprising himself—disguised as a peasant—in order to put it down and thus gain favor with the king."

"What a horrible thing to do!" Albret was pleased to have caught her interest. "I hope he is justly punished," she continued. "People died—husbands, fathers, brothers. And many more wounded. Even you were wounded." She touched his sleeve covering the scar. "Does it still give you pain?"

Albret, though tempted to enjoy her sympathy, answered, "Only a little stiffness. Nothing to be concerned about. Yes, it was a horrible, disgusting thing that the conte did. Apparently, the Duke of Lerma agreed, because he levied on him a heavy fine. And certainly he will not be invited to be one of the king's grandees and live at court."

"Well, I'm glad he was not rewarded for his foolishness." She rose to go. "Thank you, Albret, for sharing this with me. It's like we were back in Terni when we kept no secrets from each other."

Albret stood and took her hand. "It need not be just a fond memory—our talking together. There is more I want to tell you. More that will bring us closer. . .to the fulfillment of our goal. I love you, Anabella, but—"

She let go of his hand and crossed her arms as though she were scolding a child—the moments of romantic intimacy shattered. "Albret, when a man truly loves a woman, he commits to her. Asks for a betrothal. We are still young, and I would expect to wait for the consummation in marriage. But love itself is either there or it is not. You rescinded our betrothal—and for what? So you've now proved your honor and your worth. You say you love me, *but*. . . But what?"

Her uncharacteristic words stunned him, and her tears tore down his defenses. "Anabella, I do love you, and I wish to renew our betrothal. Although I must leave tomorrow to report to Captain Gaza, I am ready to commit to you now. But there is something else I need to tell you."

She burst into sobs and buried her face on his chest. He held her close, not knowing how to handle this. He had expected a joyful reunion. The news of the purse, he now knew, would have no great value for her. He would not mention it.

"Something else you have to do before committing?" With her arms circled around him, she looked up into his face. Her eyes seemed to plead for reassurance. "What is it?"

"I have been challenged to a duel of honor."

She released him and stepped back. With a handkerchief pulled from her sleeve, she blotted her eyes. "You refused, did you not?"

"I would have been labeled a coward if I had refused." He dared not mention the word *honor*. "It will probably take place in early spring, and it would greatly please me if you were there to witness my win."

"To witness your being sliced to pieces right before my eyes! I think not." She turned quickly, her skirts swirling, and headed toward the door.

"Wait, Anabella. We have not agreed on the particulars, such as the measure of the win. We will probably sword fight only to first blood drawn. I'm sorry. . . ."

She stopped in the doorway and looked back at him.

"I only thought you should know about the duel before we commit our love to each other." He stood with his hands outstretched.

But she did not run to him. Instead, she said over her shoulder, "Your commitment comes too late, Albret. Excuse me, I have a dress to make." And she slipped away from him.

thirteen

Anabella awoke early the next morning. The rain had stopped during the night, but from her window, she could see that the sky remained overcast. She had scarcely seen Albret since their emotional conversation in the receiving room the previous morning. He had spent much of the day modeling for Bianca's sketch of Joseph. She had stopped by to observe a time or two but, not wishing to disturb Bianca's concentration, had simply nodded at him and left.

Listlessly she went about her toilet and dressed for the day, her emotions jumbled together in turmoil. She thought of the New Year's Eve ball where it seemed that Frederico had cast a spell over her. He had actually asked her to marry him! Clarice might have reported the kiss on the terrace to her mother, but she herself had revealed nothing. She did not recall his exact words— but there could be no doubt it was a proposal. *And I think I said, "I don't know." Yet he seemed to assume I already belonged to him. He even introduced me to a friend of his as "my lovely Anabella."*

With chagrin, she recalled his intention to write to her brother Marco in Terni, asking for the impalmare agreement. *Oh, what have I done!* And then there was Albret. His ambivalence had peeved her. The reprimand she had thrown at him in the receiving room had been brewing for some time. He deserved it! Then just as he was ready for commitment, he had to announce his participation in a duel. The thought of dueling repulsed her.

What can I ever do to untangle myself from this double plight I have plunged my life into? Suddenly an idea struck her that would solve—or at least diminish—her duel problems. She hurried down the hall to Papa Antonio's study, where he kept his writing paper, quills, and sealing wax.

Albret and Massetti had just packed their horses and returned to say their parting remarks in the entrance hall. When Anabella arrived, Albret was in the process of distributing gifts. He had just handed his mother and Bianca small tin boxes of perfumed powder tied with ribbon. He kissed his mother, Signora Maseo, on both cheeks and hugged her. "When will you two grace the Biliverti castle again?" he asked. "Will you stay here until the painting is finished?"

"Yes, I would like to complete it before returning," said Bianca. "Probably in early summer. And thank you for the Epiphany gift. How very thoughtful of you."

"I found them in the markets in Pisa. And Signora Turati, here is a bag of presents for the children. They are figures to begin their own presepios. The *Santo Bambino* is for Gian."

"They will love them, Albret!" she said.

"We will be visiting all the children who have been placed on Epiphany or the day after. I thank you for thinking of them," said Papa Antonio.

Anabella stood shyly back from the group until Albret noticed her. "Anabella, I thought I would not see you. . .again. I have something for you also." He blushed. "I've already returned it to my saddlebag. Could you. . .would you wait a moment while I retrieve it?"

"Yes, Albret, I will wait for you," she said.

As soon as he was out of sight, Anabella's mother said, "Perhaps he intends to reinstate your betrothal. Has he mentioned anything to you?"

Anabella simply shook her head. Their words on the subject had been too complicated to explain even if she had wished to do so.

"We all have an interest, you know," said Bianca. "Sylvia, what do you think are your son's intentions?"

"That is not for me to say," Bianca's attendant said. "As you know, I am quite fond of Anabella, but I understand his—"

Albret returned carrying a black velvet bag slightly larger than the size of his hand and tied with a golden drawstring. "I bought this in Pisa from an artisan who was making them, Anabella. For you." He handed it to her while everyone stood silently and watched. "It's a piece for your family's presepio. You said you were just beginning to expand your set."

Anabella felt ill at ease with all eyes upon her as she held the little black bag in both hands. No doubt he had intended to present it to her yesterday when they were alone. She reached inside and gently withdrew the painted wooden piece.

"A villa," she whispered. "You bought me a villa."

"Notice the signora in the window upstairs with the open shutters," said Albret, pointing out the figure. "She is waving to—"

"To the signore on horseback below." Anabella completed his sentence. "Thank you, Albret. It's beautiful. I'll set it on my dressing table so I can enjoy it the whole year before it joins the rest of the presepio." His thoughtfulness touched her heart, but she wondered why he had squandered his meager means to purchase all the expensive gifts. And why a villa?

The others crowded around to admire the gift and, she felt, to speculate on the meaning of it. Did it seem obvious to all that the villa symbolized their future together? Or did they see it simply as a nice Epiphany gift?

She passed the object around so all could admire the details. Then she pulled a folded and sealed paper from her sleeve. "Albret, would you be so kind as to deliver this letter to my brother?" She handed it to him. "Tell Marco we all love and miss him."

"Of course. I am happy to do so." He smiled down at her warmly and touched her shoulder, but they silently agreed to no good-bye kiss, not in front of everyone, not with all the uncertainty. "I will put it with the letters your mother and Bianca gave to me earlier," he said.

Massetti opened the double front doors, bowed as Albret

walked through them, and the two men were off amid shouts of *arrivederci*.

≈

"We will focus on the use of rapiers made of flexible Italian steel as you requested," said Pierre de Malherbe, the fencing master Albret had hired. Rather than go directly to the Biliverti castle, he had inquired at the local tavern in Terni about instructors. Without reservation, Malherbe was declared the best in the region.

"Choose whichever appeals to you," said Malherbe, waving his hand toward a rack of foils.

Albret made his selection, but having never received formal instruction, he knew little on which to base his choice. He slipped his hand onto the grip and wrapped his finger over the cross-guard.

"Not a bad choice, Albret. But you may place the sword here on the table while dressing. Put on this padded plastron for your chest, leather gloves, and mask. Next time, wear soft leather boots that will help you maneuver."

"Should I not first explain my purpose. . .my situation?" Albret protested.

"Foremost, I need to evaluate your present skill." The master smiled indulgently. "After one bout, you can explain your goals, and I'll decide if you are capable of reaching them." The man appeared nearly three times Albret's age, with a drooping gray mustache and well-trimmed beard. Stooped and shorter than Albret, he moved slowly.

"That's sensible," said Albret as he put on the paraphernalia given him. When finished, he looked up and saw Malherbe offering his right profile at the opposite end of the studio— erect as the old man could manage, feet at right angles, and the point of his sword resting on the floor. Albret picked up the foil, faced him, and imitated his stance. Both men saluted.

As they crossed swords, Albret felt tense and unsure of himself. The master's first feint, he assumed, was to test his reaction. He parried quickly and accurately. But as their swords clashed, the master increased his speed and agility, putting Albret on the defensive.

Soon, however, Albret was able to assault, engage, attack, and advance more aggressively. Then suddenly Malherbe disarmed him with a sharp blow to his blade. At the same time his weapon fell to the floor, Albret realized the buttoned tip of his opponent's foil pressed against his throat.

"Ah-ha! So this is how you sword fight, young man?" Malherbe said, retrieving the fallen foil by its blade and handing it to Albret. "You are quite precise but restricted. An influence of a French master perhaps?"

The men sat down at a small table. They removed their masks and other protective gear. Malherbe seemed winded, though he had fenced like a young man. Albret felt exhilarated. The master handed him a fresh towel from a stack on a nearby shelf and poured water from a pitcher into two tankards.

"I have never had the benefit of formal lessons by a master," said Albret, draining his tankard. "My mother served a banker in Rome, a Signore Stefano Marinelli, who spent much of his childhood in France. He it was who taught me most of what I know. His purpose, however, was not to instill in me the fine points of dueling but to train me as a personal guard for his daughter. She is presently the *Marchesa* Bianca Biliverti."

"Ah, of course, I know all three of the noble families of Terni, the Bilivertis, the Bargerinos, the—"

"Actually, I am here because of a certain Bargerino, a conte who lives in Siena but has passed some time here with his relatives."

"Could you be speaking of Conte Frederico?"

"The same," said Albret with some surprise. "Do you know him well?"

"Indeed, I do. He took lessons from me as a youth one summer," said Malherbe. "As I recall, he would only practice with partners younger or less skilled than himself. He came here recently for a few lessons just before he led that effort to squelch a peasants' rebellion. I hear he lost, poor fellow. Probably stayed behind the ranks rather than lead."

"He has challenged me to a duel of honor, Malherbe."

"Whatever for?" the master said, slapping his knee with amusement.

"I foolishly called him a coward," Albret admitted.

"That's comical," said Malherbe, almost choking with laughter. "But you are not a nobleman. Why would he challenge someone of inferior status? That is certainly craven and not even honorable."

"When his second made the challenge, he was under the impression that I was a relative of the Bilivertis. I am the overseer of their vast seigniory, and he must have assumed. . ."

"So you accepted the challenge?"

"The marchese says I should not have, but I felt it dishonorable to refuse."

The master refilled both tankards and waited several seconds before giving a response. "Yes, of course, a man must defend his honor. Had you refused, he may have hired bandits to do you in. The conte is the one who should be regretting his words. There will be little honor for him in defeating a commoner. He had expressed to me that he wished to win a duel to enhance his reputation." Malherbe suppressed a chuckle behind his hand.

Then he suddenly became quite solemn. "Albret, I was prepared to tell you that I could have you in fine shape as a swordsman in a couple of years or so. But you probably do not have that sort of time."

"In four days I am to send a second to meet a Signore Guillermo Vasco at the crossroads here in Terni," said Albret, embarrassed that he knew no one to speak for him as his second. "They are to draw up the agreement, and the duel most likely will take place in early spring."

"So a couple of months instead of a couple of years. You ask a lot of an old man." He looked down and shook his head.

Albret felt panic seize him. He had no alternative plan if the master refused him. "But Malherbe, the fellows at the inn speak highly of you. 'He's a man of honor and resourcefulness who will rise to almost any challenge,' they told me. Also that you had been a famous instructor at the Academy of Arms in Paris."

Albret saw the old man's eyes brighten. "Yes, those were good days. But since I have settled here, I have come to admire the freedom of movement in the Italian style. That is what you must learn. Be less constrained, Albret. Feel the emotion rise in your blood!"

"Then you will take me on as your student?" Albret could not conceal his eagerness.

"You are a challenge, young man. But why not? I thrive on challenges." He stood, as did Albret, and shook his hand. "Tomorrow at two of the clock for your first lesson."

"A final question before I depart, Malherbe," said Albret, boldly looking him in the eye. "Do you know of someone appropriate to serve as my second?"

"Well, he should be someone of your social class. You cannot ask the Marchese Biliverti." He rubbed his bearded chin. "Though a commoner, you have the bearing of a gentleman, apparently a man of means. Do you not have a friend among your peers whose skill with the sword equals—or surpasses—your own?"

Albret had already considered his fellow soldiers in combat, such as Massetti, but valiantly as they had fought, they lacked more of the art of dueling than himself. "There is no one," he said.

"Then I must take it on!" Malherbe said with exuberance. "I've heard of this Vasco fellow, the conte's second. And it would be a pleasure to see Frederico defeated. That will be my incentive to produce a miracle in you."

"Thank you, Malherbe. I will work hard not to disappoint you." He pumped the master's hand vigorously. "Until tomorrow."

fourteen

Albret remained at the inn another night. On the way from Florence, he had delivered one bag of silver coins to Captain Gaza as well as the document that spelled out the king's decision for the peasants. Both bags, when Albret received them from the emissary, had been fastened with a collar and sealed with the king's insignia. At the Terni inn, alone in his room, he broke the seal of his bag and poured the contents on the floor. When he finished counting the stacks of coins, he returned to the bag all but a few pieces that he needed to pay for his room, other immediate necessities, and fencing lessons.

He lay across the bed, hands behind his head. *There is enough here to purchase a large expanse of land. And someday I will build a villa for Anabella—if she will still have me.*

Albert spent the next morning purchasing a pair of soft leather boots as Malherbe had suggested. But his afternoon fencing lesson went badly. Afterward as he rode along toward his destination, the Biliverti castle, he reviewed the master's words: "Technique is vital; you must master the moves. Intellectually, you are a good student, so you will learn all this quickly. But it's the fire inside you that must spur you on. You must read your opponent, perceive his next move. You must *feel* it and respond instantly."

He thought of Anabella. The duel had perturbed her. Though he had not sought it, if he were victorious, he could present himself as a man who had successfully defended his honor.

She had accepted his little villa replica. He had planned to give it to her earlier when they could discuss a future together. Now that he had proven himself and possessed a significant amount of money, he could recommit to the betrothal. Only the ceremony itself must wait until after the duel. For if he lost, his shame would prevent their marriage. Certainly she would understand the logic of that.

He could see the large Biliverti castle looming ahead at the top of the hill against the pale winter sky. And descending the slope, a single rider approached him.

"Buona sera," the man said and touched his hat as they passed each other. Albret also bid the stranger a good afternoon. Briefly he wondered about the man's purpose, then dismissed it. He was eager to return to his duties as overseer, as the marchese had indicated his need for his services.

Spurring his horse to a gallop, he soon arrived at the gate and handed the reins to a groom. He declined any help with his baggage, which included the heavy bag of pesos.

No one but servants stirred inside, and they paid him little mind beyond polite greetings. He took his belongings to his old room by the kitchen. While recovering from his wound, he had been pampered in one of the upstairs guest rooms. The marchese might again offer him better accommodations—considering his newly acclaimed honor in successful negotiations. The marchese seemed no longer to hold a grudge about the withdrawn betrothal when they met in Florence.

After refreshing his appearance, Albret stepped from his room with the intention of finding a bite to eat in the kitchens. The open area also led to the salon and the grand staircase. He hummed a merry tune, happy to be home again.

Abruptly, the clomping of heavy boots descending the wide staircase broke the calm. He looked up to see the marchese himself land at the foot of the stairs, red faced, and waving what appeared to be a letter.

"I saw you arrive at the front gate a few moments ago, Albret," the marchese said breathing heavily. He folded the papers and stuffed them inside his doublet. "We never know when we make a foolish decision what it will lead to, do we?" He spoke directly in Albret's face, causing him to step back.

"I—I regret bringing this duel on myself, but as I've said—"

"That was another foolish decision, but I'm referring to what you have done to my sister," he said, his anger obviously rising.

"But Marchese, I have always treated Anabella with the utmost respect and honor—"

"Do you consider it honorable to break her sweet heart by withdrawing your love? By telling her she may seek another? Answer me, young man!"

Startled by the rekindling of the issue, Albret said in defense, "I love Anabella with all my heart and recently told her so. I was at the point of recommitting my love when I returned from Pisa." Albret felt the need to bolster his stature. "Perhaps you have not heard that King Philip has sided with the peasants' cause. The meeting with his emissary in Pisa proved quite successful. It was an honor—"

"Albret, sometimes I think you confuse honor with personal glory!" the marchese said and then seemed to grow calmer. "So you won on the battlefield *and* with diplomacy. Yes, that is commendable, and I want to hear the details of the meeting. But right now, as you can see, I am extremely upset about a letter I have just received from—well, I will leave the man's name anonymous. Come, let's sit down and talk."

The little alcove next to the kitchen where Albret and Anabella used to meet was close by. The marchese sat on a bench beneath a window, and Albret took a chair on the other side of a small table.

What man? What letter? Albret's need to defend himself quickly turned to concern for Anabella. And what had he himself done to bring on the marchese's wrath?

A kitchen maid walked by carrying dishes to the dining area for the evening meal. "Signorina," said the marchese, "please bring us some tea." He leaned his elbow on the round table that sat between them and lowered his voice. "I have just received a letter from a messenger—perhaps you met him leaving as you arrived. Albret, it's from a certain gentleman asking for Anabella's hand in marriage."

Albret felt the blood drain from his face. He opened his mouth in shock but found no words to express the jolt he felt. *So that is what Anabella meant by "your commitment comes too late." She had already committed her love to another*. "I did not know," he said in a nearly inaudible voice.

"He wants their impalmare drawn up immediately—and the betrothal and wedding ceremonies both completed by summer. That is extremely fast, even for a girl nearly sixteen." The marchese paused. "I see this causes you pain, but I surmise poor Anabella has suffered much pain by your indecision."

"I am sorry for that," said Albret, burying his head in his hands, his elbows resting on the table. "I thought she would be patient. I wanted to be worthy of her love."

The marchese shook his head. "Love isn't something to be earned. But, I need to tell you the rest. He says he loves Anabella and will consider her an asset in his life. Then he has the impropriety to ask about the amount of her dowry before we have even talked. I find that offensive."

"Does he say she loves him?" Albret grasped for some hope.

"I had not intended to mention that, but, yes, Albret, he says she has declared her undying love for him and wishes to marry as soon as expedient."

"I see."

"You should never have released her to seek another. I blame you for that. If her mother and I thought you were worthy, you should have accepted our assessment. I know, you are like all the young gentlemen today. You think you have to prove yourself to be honorable."

Before honor is humility. The words rang in Albret's head. "It's hard to change one's way of thinking. I thought I was doing something *for* Anabella, not *against* her."

The maid brought a tray of cups and a kettle of herbal tea and set them on the table. She filled the two cups, bowed, and exited to the kitchen. The marchese sipped his tea and then said, "I may choose to reject this man's proposal. But in any case, I believe we should rescind the impalmare agreement between you and my family."

"As you wish, signore," Albret said with reluctance. "May I ask if you have ever met this man?"

"Yes, I have."

Albret refrained from asking more.

"I'm sure Anabella is aware the man has contacted me, and she will no doubt write—"

"Marchese, she has, indeed, already written." Albret stood, suddenly realizing what topic the sealed letter from Anabella concerned. "I have three letters for you."

৯

The following days, Albret supervised the permanent workers who remained over the winter. Repairs to outbuildings, corrals, and wine-making equipment had waited for his return. Tools and sheep shears needed sharpening. With an assistant, Albret inventoried all the animals—horses, cattle, sheep, and goats.

Thrice a week after his chores, he met with Malherbe for his lesson, and every night he practiced his dueling techniques. He would repeat one move over and over in front of a mirror propped up next to a whale-oil lamp until he perfected it. Then he would work on another—review, repeat, perfect.

Tonight he must meet the fencing master—not only for his lesson, but also to hear from Malherbe how the meeting with Guillermo Vasco had gone. The two seconds were to have met at noon at the crossroads in Terni.

The marchese had said nothing further to him about Anabella's proposal. And equally disturbing, he had not mentioned the contents of her letter. The marchese remained cool and businesslike, but anger seemed to simmer beneath the surface.

Albret changed into his gentleman's clothes and pulled on his new soft leather boots. He extinguished the lamp and slipped out of his room, closing the door quietly behind him.

"Good evening, Albret."

Startled, Albret turned to see the marchese standing beside him.

"I was on my way to knock on your door," the marchese said, quickly scanning his overseer from hat to new boots. "As I see you are on your way out, I won't keep you long. I thought you would want to know what Anabella wrote to me."

"Indeed, I do. If you would be so kind as to share her words with me." He had not told the marchese about the fencing lessons or the meeting of seconds, and he did not wish to do so. Certainly it was not necessary to explain his activities, yet he felt embarrassed to be thus intercepted. He tried to prepare his heart to hear Anabella's pledge of love to another man and the request for her brother to grant a new impalmare.

"I am angry at both of them, this man and Anabella," said the marchese. "And of course, I remain displeased with you as well, but I have already expressed that."

Albret drew in a deep breath and awaited the words that would finish tearing his heart to tatters.

"Bianca and I have always been very forward looking, often taking nontraditional positions. For example, as you know, we supported the peasants, though secretly. In Rome, my wife bravely struggled to become a recognized artist, a career generally reserved for men. I supported her choice. Bianca and I fell in love. Only afterward did our parents agree."

Albret could see no relevance to the letter in the marchese's speech.

"After other suitors proved undesirable and it became obvious that Anabella cared for you, I approached you, a man I considered of noble character. And yes, even honorable. Now we have this abominable situation."

"Marchese, could you tell me what Anabella said?" He nervously fingered the hilt of his dress sword.

"I'm getting to that," the marchese said with a sigh. "First I want you to know what I have decided about this situation.

I have come to believe that the traditional way is best. Young people do not know their own minds. Anabella is confused about love, changing her affection without thoughtful consideration. You may be steadfast in your love, but you are confused nonetheless about how to pursue it."

"You have made my errors perfectly clear. Please—"

"Anabella says she still loves you alone."

Albret could not conceal his joy.

"I know that is what you hoped to hear, Albret, but you cannot expect to depend upon it. She claims to have been smitten by this. . .this person. Apparently, he charmed her. You certainly gave her reason to open herself to the flattery of another."

"I deeply regret that, signore."

"Consider our agreement broken. I will rescind the impalmare as soon as time permits. Also, I will reject this new proposal and begin a search of my own for a proper husband. She will have no say in the matter. Now, if you will please excuse me. Good night."

Stunned by this information, Albret stood as if frozen in place for several seconds, then hurried out to the stables and saddled his horse. He hoped Malherbe had been able to negotiate a duel to first blood, not to the death. Yet did it really matter? It was small comfort that Anabella still loved him. She had, for a time, considered another man and—as the marchese implied—could do so again.

&

Albret arrived at Malherbe's studio at precisely the appointed hour. He dismounted, tied his horse, and thumped the round brass knocker thrice. After a few seconds, the master opened the door. "Punctual, that's good. Come in, Albret."

Instead of going directly to the fencing studio as they had done before, Malherbe led him to a small sitting area. The room was sparsely furnished with three wooden chairs around a square table that supported a large burning candle. In the shadows, Albret noticed a straight, narrow stairway, which he presumed led to the man's sleeping quarters. On his second visit, Albret had learned that Malherbe's wife had died before he came to Italy some ten years previously.

After both were seated at the table, Malherbe said, "I believe you will be pleased with the dueling accord. If not, we will renegotiate tomorrow at the same time. Either way, I must meet Vasco to let him know. Frederico is lodging with his relatives here in Terni, so Vasco will also have his response."

"Go on." At this point, Albret neither dreaded nor welcomed the particulars. They were merely the framework in which he would fight this duel that now, more than ever, he must win. He was eager to get on with the lesson and let physical activity calm his battered emotions.

"First of all, Conte Frederico requested that you present him with a written apology for your error in judgment by calling him a coward. And in exchange he would withdraw his challenge to duel."

Albret thought he detected a sneer at the corner of the master's mouth—perhaps a suppression of laughter. Surprised by the request, he said, "Why do you think he wants an apology? And why withdraw the challenge?"

"Because Conte Frederico *is* a coward." This time he was unable to control a chuckle as he added, "Vasco has, no doubt, told him you are not a Biliverti nor of any kind of noble blood. Even a win would be worthless to him."

Albret, devastated by his loss of Anabella, had begun to think of the duel as an escape from his sorrows. "And if I refuse to apologize, he cannot honorably withdraw the challenge. Am I right, master?"

"Exactly. So what do you wish to do?"

"You are a wise man and certainly more familiar with the Code Duello than I. What do you advise?" Albret, with his arms on the table, leaned toward Malherbe and looked him straight in the eye. He knew what the marchese would say, but after their last conversation, he preferred this man's opinion.

"Since you seek my advice, Albret, I will tell you what I would do. I would make him fight the duel he has asked for. You are already making some progress in skill. I know Frederico's weaknesses, having worked with him myself. If you accept the agreement, in two months, I can have you prepared to be the better swordsman. And in addition, you will have humiliated him for challenging someone beneath him. Thus you would hand him a double loss."

"Then that is what I shall do!" Albret pounded his fist on the table to emphasize his decision.

"Good. I told Vasco I thought that would be your answer. He must have expected the same, for he was ready to propose the place, time, and date."

"Which are?"

"There is a rounded hill," he said, "that spans the boundary between the Biliverti property and the Bargerino relatives' estate, just south of the river. It is an open area but secluded by surrounding trees, thus unlikely to be detected by authorities. He suggested that spot on the property line, which I thought proper."

"I know the area. However, the marchese does not approve of my dueling at all. He might object to a duel on his seigniory."

"Then we can move the duel entirely to the Bargerino side." Malherbe's quick response led Albret to conclude that the master had thought through all possible objections.

"And you made it clear that the conflict must end with this duel with no family feud to follow."

"Indeed, I did."

"And the date and time?"

"As you proposed, at sunrise on 15 March."

"And the measure of the win?"

"To first blood drawn or until one is disarmed." Malherbe grinned. "Remember, we are dealing with a known coward."

"Agreed on all points," said Albret.

fifteen

"I have made some terrible mistakes, Bianca," lamented Anabella. She sat on a stool in the unfinished ballroom, posing for her sister-in-law, who was sketching her as Dinah, the daughter of Jacob and Leah. Her mother and Papa Antonio had already sat for their roles as the patriarch and his first wife.

"Could you turn a bit to the right, Anabella? That's it. And place your hand on the arm of the chair. In the painting, that will be a child's shoulder. What terrible mistakes?"

"I love only Albret and no other," Anabella said hesitantly.

"Yes, I believe that. But I don't know how, after the way he has shunned you. I've known Albret all my life. I cannot even remember when he first came to live with my family in Rome. He has all the same fine qualities as his mother—loyalty, honesty, and piety. Well, perhaps not as much piety. Could you remove your shoes, Anabella? And cross your ankles. I can add the sandals later." She continued to draw.

"You were saying about Albret. . . ."

"Albret is a good man. I admire the way he has struggled to educate himself beyond my father's instruction. Marco enjoys discussing science and philosophy with him. But perhaps he has been overinfluenced by the stories he reads of ancient heroes. He aspires to the ideal—to perfection in himself." Bianca sketched the folds of a sheet that draped from Anabella's shoulder and fell gracefully toward the floor. "What about your mistakes?"

Albret's mother appeared at the doorway. "Would the signora and signorina care for tea?"

"Yes, Sylvia, we are ready for a rest," said Bianca. She wiped charcoal from her hands with a cloth and removed her smock.

119

As soon as her attendant had left the room, she turned toward Anabella. "Why don't we ask Sylvia to sit with us? She will keep a confidence and never repeat a word."

"You will both hate me, I'm afraid," said Anabella, removing the sheet and slipping on a dressing gown. She folded the sheet and laid it on the stool. Up to this point, only one settee and two chairs had been crafted and upholstered in the fabric Anabella had chosen. She sat in one chair, and Bianca settled on the settee.

Albret's mother returned with a small tray and two cups of steaming tea. As no tables were yet available, the women each took and held a saucer with cup.

"We would like you to sit with us awhile, Signora Maseo," said Anabella cordially. "Bring a cup for yourself from the kitchen."

"As you wish, signorina." The servant bowed slightly and exited.

"I've addressed her as Signora Maseo since the recording of the impalmare. It would hardly be seemly to revert to her given name," said Anabella. Then to get the words in before Albret's mother returned, she quickly added, "Bianca, another man has crossed my life. Does that shock you? Will that shock his mother?" Anabella's cup rattled on the saucer. She took a sip to prevent its spilling.

Bianca opened her mouth to answer, but Signora Maseo returned with her tea and sat down. "Is there something you wish to discuss with me?" she asked, looking from one to the other.

"I think Anabella has a dilemma," said Bianca. "We thought your wisdom might help."

"Well, I've been counseling you since you were a child, signora," she said with a smile. "I'll do my best by Signorina Anabella."

"Not a dilemma really," said Anabella, her nervousness dissipated by Signora Maseo's warmth and Bianca's apparent acceptance. "Signora Maseo, you know I love your son with all my heart, even after he released me from the betrothal."

"Yes, and he has never stopped loving you or being faithful to you alone," Signora Maseo said with a frown, as if not understanding how there could be a problem.

"I know. But I have let another man come into my life. I've seen him on only a few occasions, always chaperoned." She paused, expecting words of reproof, but both women seemed merely to be listening attentively. "I admit that he fascinated me, and I fell for his flattery."

"I see no harm in that," said Bianca. "Albret did release you."

Sylvia raised her eyebrows, finished her tea, and set the cup on the tray on the floor next to her chair.

"He asked me to marry him," Anabella said flatly.

Both women gasped in unison.

"I didn't give him an answer. I said he would have to write my brother because only he could make that decision. Of course, I knew Marco would let me follow my heart. He's very modern in his thinking, but I was so startled I didn't know what to say. In that moment—it was at the New Year's ball at the Uffizi—I didn't know what I wanted. Albret had seemed so distant. . . ." She confessed the rest, about writing her own letter to Marco and her reaction to the duel Albret was going to fight. She was surprised to learn they both already knew about his duel.

"No one ever tells me anything," said Anabella, choking back tears. "Not you, not mother, not Papa Antonio." She blotted her eyes with the sleeve of her dressing gown.

"That's the way society is toward young women today," said Bianca. "My parents also kept important information from me. I fought against it at your age myself, and now I am guilty of the same."

Signora Maseo got up and placed her arm around Anabella's shoulders. "And of course, as a personal attendant, I hear and see much, but I never reveal anything unless Bianca asks me directly about something. I thought it only proper for Albret to tell you himself," she said and returned to her place. Anabella thought about Clarice witnessing the kiss from Frederico— one bit of information she chose not to reveal. Clarice would not have told unless her mother had asked.

"So what do you think about Albret's dueling, Signora Maseo?" Anabella fully expected his mother to agree with her feelings—that it was a terrible and foolish thing that men do.

"I know you are repulsed by it, signorina, but I think I understand why my son feels honor-bound to accept the challenge," said Sylvia pensively. "Sometimes it is good, I think, for a woman to stand with her man, even if she does not understand the way he has chosen."

"Sylvia always offers wise advice," said Bianca. "And I cannot see that the problem with this other man is too grave, Anabella. When Marco reads your letter, he will certainly refuse his proposal. And the predicament will be solved." She set her cup on the tray and slipped on her artist's smock. "Let us all get back to work."

Signora Maseo picked up the tray, bowed, and said, "Signorina, do not give up hope. I pray for you and Albret."

"Thank you," said Anabella with a grateful smile. "I will consider your words of advice."

As soon as Sylvia had left, Bianca returned to her sketch. "I no longer need you as a model, Anabella. But by the way, who is this man so smitten by you?"

"I thought you already knew," she said. As she was on her way toward the door, she stopped and turned. "He is Conte Frederico Bargerino, whose relatives you know in Terni."

"No! That cannot be!" Bianca ran to Anabella and faced her with her hands on her shoulders. "You were taken in and nearly betrothed to the very man Albret fought against? How could you do that, Anabella?" No longer was Bianca the forgiving and understanding sister-in-law.

Just as Bianca began to shake Anabella's shoulders, the room swirled and she remembered nothing more.

❧

Anabella opened her eyes to see a crowd of anxious faces looking down at her—Bianca, Sylvia, Clarice, and even Papa Antonio. Her mother knelt beside her, bathing her face with a cold cloth. She shivered in spite of a blanket that had been tucked around her. Someone pushed a cushion under her head.

"Wh–where am I?"

"You are here at home with your family who loves you," said Papa Antonio, squeezing her hand.

"I am so sorry, Anabella," said Bianca with a grief-stricken face. "It was my fault. I should not have said what I did. I was just so shocked."

The words came back to her. She closed her eyes as Bianca's voice repeated in her memory: *"Betrothed to the very man Albret fought against."*

"Bianca, I–I never knew Frederico was the conte that Albret fought. I wouldn't do that, Signora Maseo. . . Mother. . ." She could read in their faces that they all had just heard the story about her and the conte on New Year's Eve.

"We should have told you," her mother said, tears glistening in her eyes. "We never thought you would see him again."

"We are sorry," said Papa Antonio. "Let me help you up."

❧

Anabella spent the next few days in her room, disheartened and distressed. The first day she escaped into sleep but awakened often, filled with anger, especially at her mother and Papa Antonio, who knew all along who the conte was— or at least knew after a certain point. Not only had they concealed the fact from her, but they had requested Frederico not contact her—leaving her in ignorance. After much prayer, she conceded they intended no harm and only meant to protect her. They seemed truly sorry, and by the second day, she forgave them.

Later when Clarice brought her breakfast tray, Anabella sat up in bed and said, "You never told my parents about my dancing at the ball or about the kiss, did you, Clarice?"

"No, signorina," Clarice said, shaking her head. "I did not know he was the conte who incited the peasants' rebellion. Nor did I know that he was forbidden to see you. I only report something to your mother if she asks specifically. I suppose I should have told her the conte pursued you at the ball. Perhaps that would have spared you some pain."

"Well, at least I'm not the only one left in ignorance." She smiled at her mother's attendant. "You did exactly what you should have done."

Once Anabella had forgiven everyone else, her own guilt engulfed her. She should not have been so foolish. The romantic evening had been overpowering, but that was no excuse. Why hadn't she rebuffed Frederico outright? She never should have suggested he write to Marco. To think she had danced with Albret's enemy! Innocence of his identity did not lessen the remorse. And instead of rebuffing Frederico, she had turned away Albret, the man she truly loved. From her bed, she looked at the miniature villa on her dressing table that Albret had given her, at the happy couple waving at each other. *A lost and unreal dream*, she thought.

On the morning of the fifth day, she got up, bathed, and dressed. In the little chapel, she knelt and asked God for forgiveness and strength to return to daily life. She prayed for discernment, for surely she had fallen short in that regard. She arose feeling forgiven and renewed. Descending the staircase, she met Signora Maseo bringing a tray up to her.

"You look lovely this morning, signorina," Albret's mother said, beaming. "Everyone will be so pleased to see you at the breakfast table." She turned around and followed Anabella down the stairs. "Bianca plans to sketch little Pietro this morning. You won't want to miss that!"

≈

Anabella's spirits lifted in the following days as she watched her design for the ballroom take form. The blue drapery with a subtle leaf pattern had been delivered and hung; the rest of the baroque-style chairs and tables arrived; the famous Guido Reni agreed to decorate the vaulted ceiling with frescos; and Papa Antonio's business partner brought back a selection of tapestries from Vienna. She chose—with opinions from the others—a hunting scene for one wall and the baptism of Christ by St. John the Baptist for the opposite wall. Bianca's painting would hang on the south wall across from windows that let in an abundance of light.

The height of excitement came with the arrival of the sculptor who had been commissioned for the statues. He brought two small maquettes in clay for approval before continuing in marble.

He set the models on one of the tables in the ballroom. "This is the Good Shepherd carrying a lost lamb across his shoulders," said the sculptor, a slender man in midlife. "It is a popular theme as I'm sure you know. But mine is somewhat unique. See, the lamb is struggling against being saved. Like most of humankind." He looked around to see the family's reaction.

"It's wonderful!" said Anabella's mother. "What do you think, Anabella?"

"It's beyond my expectations," she said, imagining the figure life-size in marble. "And this must be St. John the Baptist with his camel-hair cloak and uplifted hand, preaching."

"Yes. Signore Turati had suggested Old Testament characters to go with the painting, but since you left which ones up to me, I decided on these from the New Testament. I can change them of course."

"No, I think we all embrace your idea, signore," said Bianca.

"And what a fine painting you are creating, *Marchesa* Biliverti," the sculptor—and longtime acquaintance of Bianca—said, waving his arm toward the canvas, which sat propped up on two easels. Bianca had applied the undercoats and transferred her sketched figures to the larger canvas. She had almost completed the oil portraits of Jacob and Leah.

"Thank you, my friend," she said.

The sculptor looked around the ballroom. "And where, may I ask, did you find a master artist to design the whole of this? It's extraordinarily harmonious. Each artist can do what he does best, but without someone to see the entirety, it will be a calamity. My clients often ask if I know someone who can design interiors such as this. So would you mind sharing his name?"

Anabella put her hand to her mouth to suppress a giggle. Her mother and Papa Antonio exchanged surprised looks.

"Perhaps I am being indiscreet to ask."

"No, not at all," said Bianca. "We are proud to divulge the name. *She* is our own Signorina Anabella Biliverti!"

Anabella felt her face flush. Nevertheless, the praise pleased her. She bowed and said, "I am the designer, signore."

The sculptor, flustered by the surprise of a mere girl possessing such art, stammered. "Unbelievable. . . How is it possible? . . . I am impressed. But—but, why not? The *marchesa* is a lauded painter. I may even recommend you myself."

"We are all proud of her," said Papa Antonio.

After the man packed up his maquettes and left, they all had a hearty laugh.

"Someday," said Bianca in a more serious tone, "women may be accepted in whatever field they choose without being a curiosity."

"What if he does recommend me?" said Anabella. The thought of being paid for doing what she loved never before had occurred to her.

"We'll discuss that possibility when and if it happens," said Papa Antonio. "Meanwhile, we will just enjoy your talent ourselves."

sixteen

"Parry, engage, break. . .feint, more quickly, withdraw. Avoid flourishes." The long, narrow fencing studio appeared unsettling at night. Sconces with lit candles interspersed between long mirrors lined one wall and cast moving shadows of the actors. The room lay silent save for the clash of steel and the occasional grunt or words of instruction.

"Come in close. Protect yourself. Thrust. Not so good. All right, Albret, let's talk a bit," said Malherbe.

They took off their protective gear and sat at the small table. Albret took a towel and wiped sweat from his forehead. Though the room was unheated, the vigorous exercise had warmed him.

"I'm not making much progress, am I?" he asked with a grin and poured two tankards of water.

"You are improving," said Malherbe. "Not bad for a month of hard work on both our parts. You've mastered every technique I've given you." He ran his fingers through his thin hair and hesitated. "Do you care passionately about winning this duel, Albret?"

"I do, master." Albret felt the sting of criticism.

"It seems to me. . .well, it's like you are fencing alone in your room. The techniques are performed perfectly. But you are not reading me, your opponent. I want to see fire. Emotion and determination. Like love, it must move from the head to the heart."

Love is either there or it is not. He thought of Anabella's words, how she had come into his arms weeping. For the love of Anabella, he must win this duel. It was the last barrier. "I will try to imagine you as Frederico. For I must win."

"Good. Now remember to be efficient in movement. Always anticipate an opening for a single direct thrust. It is not a question of if it will open up, but when. Be ready and lunge." Malherbe continued with various instructions and reminded him of the new techniques he was to practice.

"Thank you, Malherbe." Albret arose and laid the agreed number of coins on the table. "Same time, night after tomorrow?"

"Yes," said the master, nodding. "By the way, I ran into Vasco at the tavern yesterday. He tells me Frederico has returned to Siena and is trying to sell his land there. Apparently he is in grave financial trouble and plans to marry a lady with a large dowry that might include some land. But all is still set for the duel on 15 March."

"Don't tell me any more about the conte's personal life. I would rather not envision him as a man touched by misfortune. Or for that matter, capable of love."

"All right. Let's turn to another topic. I have taken the liberty of ordering you a rapier of the finest steel from Toledo, created by a master craftsman."

"Good, I need a fine sword. Whatever the price, I can afford it," said Albret without hesitation. "Consider it purchased."

"I thought you would agree. And has the marchese agreed to dueling on the property line?"

"My relationship with the marchese is strained at the present time. I'm awaiting the right moment." Albret was reluctant to reveal such information, but he needed to excuse himself for not having inquired.

"We really don't have to know until we arrive on the dueling field. Frederico will be pleased to duel entirely on Bargerino land, I should think."

Malherbe scooped up the coins from the table. "Don't worry, Albret. You will be prepared when the time comes." He slapped his student on the back.

Albret rode back to the castle by moonlight, arriving around midnight. Once in his room, he immediately took out paper and quill to pen a letter to Anabella, who remained constantly on his mind.

❧

Anabella sat at her dressing table while Clarice plaited her hair in one long braid, which she coiled at the crown of her head, leaving loose tendrils to frame her face. Anabella wore the dress she had been working on the night she had reprimanded Albret for his noncommitment and objected to his fighting a duel. She still regretted letting him slip away.

"You will outshine the bride," said Clarice as she added the final touches to her hair. The beige dress was trimmed in rose and matched the velvet ribbon Clarice wrapped around the braided bun.

"Cecilia would never allow that," Anabella said with a laugh.

"I have already done up your mother's hair," said Clarice. "She and Signore Turati await you in the salon."

The family arrived in their carriage at two of the clock in the afternoon and easily found the private chapel in the duomo. Anabella stood between her parents, flanked by their servants and surrounded by about fifty other guests. A robed priest and the stout Barone di Bicci, wearing a doublet made of gold cloth, stood by the altar next to his parents.

Cecilia entered dressed in pale peach silk, a white mantilla draped over her head and crowned with a wreath of rosemary. Her parents, Simonetta, and two servant girls followed—one of which was Luisa. They took their places across from the di Biccis. Anabella caught Luisa's shy smile and thought she appeared happy in her new position.

As the wedding ceremony began, Anabella imagined herself in Cecilia's place and Albret instead of the barone. The priest led the couple in their *verba de praesenti* vows, in which they agreed "at this very moment" to be forever husband and wife. After the prayers and blessing by the priest, Cecilia's father shook the barone's hand, which sealed the commitment.

The priest then invited all present to enter the larger sanctuary of the church and join in the regular Sunday mass. Anabella, still between her parents, entered with conflicted emotions—happiness for her friend Cecilia and sadness over her own plight. Her heart ached from missing Albret. She had heard nothing from him in the six weeks since he left. Nor had she received a response from Marco.

Halfway down the aisle, she felt something touch her elbow. When she turned, a boy of about twelve handed her a rolled paper. Before she could say a word, he disappeared into the crowd. But among the wedding guests, she caught a glimpse of none other than Conte Frederico Bargerino leaning against a pillar and looking in her direction. She quickly slipped the note into her sleeve and followed her parents, who had seen nothing.

Anabella repeated the prayers and went through the litany of the mass, scarcely aware of the words. Her mind could not forget the note in her sleeve that felt like something alive and menacing. She prayed that Frederico would not approach her following the service, and for once she welcomed her parents' protection.

After the service, the guests gathered outside on the piazza to meet with the couple and wish them well. Simonetta and Visconte Carlo Strozzi chatted vivaciously.

On the arm of her beloved, Cecilia approached Anabella. "Of course you will come to our villa for the meal and celebration," said the bride.

"Please forgive me, Cecilia. I am enduring a severe headache and must return home. But my parents will be there," said Anabella, who did indeed suffer from a headache as well as the constant fear of encountering the conte.

"Oh, I'm so disappointed." Cecilia pushed out her lower lip in a pout. "We've invited Conte Frederico. He will certainly want to see you."

"Really, Cecilia, I cannot. But I wish you and Romolo all

the happiness that you so rightly deserve," she said, her eyes darting around to find her parents, who had momentarily left her side.

"We will expect you and Frederico to visit us soon," said Romolo graciously.

Frederico? They think of us as a couple? Quickly excusing herself, she found her mother and explained her headache and need to leave.

"You do appear pale," said her mother, touching her cheek and frowning. "But no fever. Antonio, we can leave in the carriage now, let off Anabella at our villa, and still arrive in time for the celebration. Don't you think so?"

"Of course. We don't want any more fainting spells," said Papa Antonio. "Bianca and Sylvia are there and will watch after her."

ਦੇ

Finally home in her own room, Anabella withdrew the scroll of paper from her sleeve and flung it on her dressing table as if it were a burning object. She undressed quickly, donned her nightclothes, and unwound her hair. Just as she picked up the scroll and sat down on her bed to determine what she had been given, a knock came at the door. She quickly tucked the paper under her covers and called, "Come in."

It was Signora Maseo carrying a tray. "You complained of a headache, Signorina Anabella. I've made you some willow bark tea." She set the tray on the dressing table and brought her the cup. "This should ease your pain." She turned to go.

"Please stay, Signora Maseo."

"Is there something more you need?"

"I need. . .I need you to stay with me awhile. Please, sit down." Signora took a chair next to the bed and folded her hands. Anabella noted that the older woman's handsome profile strongly resembled that of her son's. Her hair, graying at the temples, was pulled back in a roll at the nape of her neck. "I want to talk to you. . .as a friend. . .and as Albret's mother," said Anabella.

"Well, I think I can fit easily into both of those roles." She patted Anabella's hand and smiled at her. "You know whatever you say will not be shared."

"I know, and I thank you for that." She sipped the tea and tucked her bare feet under her. "Mother and Papa Antonio are very protective, and right now I need that. But something happened at the wedding that I didn't want to share with them."

"Is that what brought on the headache?"

"I suppose. At least that is why I needed to come home." She started to hand the empty cup to signora, but right now she didn't wish to think of her as an attendant. Instead, she hopped off the bed and placed the cup on the tray herself. When she sat down again, she wrapped a blanket around her shoulders and looked at Albret's mother. "If you are cold, signora," Anabella offered, "I can get you a blanket, too."

"Thank you, Anabella, but I am comfortable and dressed warmly."

"I saw Conte Frederico this afternoon." Noticing no reaction from Albret's mother, she continued. "As we were going into the church service, a boy came up behind me and handed me something. When I turned around, the conte was there in the crowd. I assume it is a note from him. I knew if I went to the celebration, he would try to talk to me. God has forgiven me my foolishness in being attracted to him, but I cannot forget that he battled against Albret and his troops. Albret was even wounded in the conflict he caused."

"So what was the message he sent you?"

It pleased Anabella that signora asked, as any friend would. "I don't know." Her eyes twinkled, and for the first time that day, she felt some mirth creep in. "Shall we find out?" She reached under the covers of her bed and drew out the tightly rolled piece of paper. With signora beside her, it no longer seemed ominous but simply mysterious. She untied the white satin ribbon that bound it and unrolled the paper.

"Whatever this is, I am going to read it aloud, signora. You are my confidant."

"I am ready," said Signora Maseo with all the calm assurance of an uninvolved bystander—and confidant.

Anabella read:

My dearest Anabella,

I have received no word from your brother, the Marchese Biliverti, *in response to my proposal. I am concerned, for I had hoped we could be wed soon. You will remember on New Year's Eve I invited you to witness my duel of honor. Since you gave no answer, I am issuing the invitation again. The duel is to take place at sunrise, 15 of March, in Terni on a knoll south of the river, on the Bargerino estate, very near the Biliverti property. I assume you visit your brother from time to time, so I trust this will be possible. Do not worry. We will fight only to first blood or disarming—and I shall be the one to first draw blood. I face an evil opponent who has no knowledge of truth. Until our* impalmare *is in place, I know your mother will object to our seeing each other. But write to me in Siena if you are able to do so. Otherwise, regardless of the* marchese's *response, I will expect you there to witness the duel—as my inspiration and courage.*

My heart belongs only to you.
Your loving Frederico

"How disgusting!" Anabella looked up, expecting to be consoled. But instead, she saw Signora Maseo bent over with her hands covering her face. "What is it, signora? You seem even more upset than I."

Signora kept her hands clasped on the sides of her face. Her eyes glistened with tears. "I just realized, Anabella. It was that horrible man—for it can be no other than Conte Bargerino—who challenged my son to a duel of honor. Albret never told me who it was, but this makes it clear. And he falsely calls my son an evil liar."

Anabella fell back distraught into the pillows on her bed and tossed the note to the floor. "In Terni, of course! He assumes I don't know who his opponent is. And we didn't until now. You know I will not go. Certainly not to be *his* inspiration."

"It is not my place to tell you this, Anabella, but he is the one who wounded Albret in battle. My son told me that."

Many emotions engulfed Anabella—anger at the conte for his assumptions, anger at Albret for concealing the name of his opponent, love for Albret, contempt for Frederico, and other feelings she could not identify. When Signora Maseo stood, Anabella got up from her bed. The two women threw their arms around each other and wept in mutual consolation.

seventeen

A few weeks later, Anabella found Bianca working alone on the huge span of canvas set on the double easels. "Do you mind if I come in and watch you for a while?" Anabella said, as she walked across the ballroom to where her sister-in-law stood absorbed in her painting. The odor of oil paint hung in the air. Bianca was just finishing the face of Joseph, modeled after Albret.

"Not at all. Pietro is sleeping, so I must concentrate fully and take advantage of the time. But your company is always welcome." Not looking up, she completed Joseph's second eyebrow with a finely pointed brush. "How do you like him?"

"You know Albret so well," said Anabella, studying the features closely. "You've captured a certain expression of his perfectly. Joseph is looking for his brothers, but Albret is searching for the man be hopes to become." His brown eyes seemed to look off in the distance, a slight frown on his brow, and his lips were parted as if about to speak her name. Anabella wished for his bodily presence and their reconciliation. "He's rather charming in his short, shepherd's robe. I like it."

Bianca continued working on his wayward locks of hair. "This painting is taking much longer than I expected," she said. "I miss Marco, and I know he misses me and Pietro." She wiped her brush on a cloth and dabbed it in a lighter brown on her palette. "I think we will go back to Terni for a few weeks and return later in the spring to finish the painting and see it framed. I've already talked to Mother Costanza about it."

"I will miss you—and Signora Maseo." Anabella tried to mask the fear of loneliness that came over her. Since sharing the note from Frederico, she had especially come to rely on Signora Maseo, who shared her concerns.

"You don't need to miss us." For the first time since Anabella had come in, Bianca paused and turned to look at her. "I also asked your mother if you could come to Terni with us. Would you like that?"

Surprised by this unforeseen opportunity to see Albret, tears stung the corners of her eyes. "Indeed, I would! Did Mother give her permission?"

"Without hesitation. Your mother worries that you have been sad of late and thinks it would be good for you. She considered coming, too, to be with her grandchild more, but she decided to stay here with Father Antonio. After all, since their marriage, he has given up traveling with his merchandising train to stay at home with her."

They both became aware of a boy, about ten, standing in the doorway, nervously fussing with some papers. When they looked at him, he stammered, "Here's something—maybe letters—for you." He held out the crumpled papers.

Anabella went to him, knelt, and hugged him. The child threw his skinny arms around her neck and only reluctantly let go when she stood up. "Thank you, Damian. Let's see—this one is for the *Marchesa* Biliverti. And this one is for me. Next time, Damian, remember to tap on the door, even if we are talking. Then you bow and say, 'Marchesa and signorina, some messages have arrived for you.' Let me hear you say that."

The child blushed and grinned but repeated the statement word for word.

"That's very good, Damian. Remember, we have lessons after lunch today. Gian will show you where."

The boy grinned again. "Yes, signorina. I will be there." He bowed correctly, turned, and left.

"I should have reminded him not to rumple messages, but I didn't wish to be too harsh. Papa Antonio found him shivering and in tatters by a bridge over the Arno River. His parents had both died some time ago, and his aunt turned him out, saying he was old enough to fend for himself. She has six children of her own it seems. Poor thing." Anabella shook her head at the child's awful plight.

"But he will mend beautifully under your parents' care—like all the others," said Bianca, placing a comforting hand on Anabella's shoulder.

"I know. And I will miss out on the beginning of his instruction, but he will do well. It gives me so much pleasure to watch them grow. By the handwriting, I see we both have letters from Marco. I will leave you to read yours in private."

❧

In her room, Anabella lay prone across her bed. With nervous fingers, she broke the seal and was surprised to see a second letter inside the first with its own seal—from Albret. Marco's was much shorter, and she read it first.

> *My dear 'Bella,*
> *Forgive me for waiting so long to write. In truth, I felt anger both toward you and Conte Frederico. You say you still love Albret, but girls your age lack steadfastness. I am content to lay aside any plans for your marriage for a while. Time heals many wounds. Next year I will begin a search in earnest for a worthy husband.*
>
> > *Your brother who loves you,*
> > *Marco*

With little emotional reaction, she laid his letter aside and turned to the one she most yearned to read. *Did Albret agree with Marco? Had she fatally pushed him away? Might he still love her?* She closed her eyes and tried to prepare herself for whatever lay therein.

> *My dear Anabella,*
> *Please believe I love you with all my heart as I always have.*

I long to see you, hold you in my arms, and tell you over and over how much you mean to me.

Recently, your brother told me that another man has sought your hand in marriage. I cannot blame you for that involvement as I released you from our betrothal. Thus the pain I suffer is of my own making.

Happily, your brother also informed me that you declined the other man's proposal of marriage. He did not offer to give me your letter, but he quoted your words that you love me alone. I hope and pray that is still your feeling.

As you know, I face a duel of honor. Like you, the marchese *does not approve of my acceptance of the challenge. But after many discussions and debates with your brother, he has come to an understanding of my position. Though he does not agree, he has pledged not to oppose me in doing what I consider honorable and necessary. I hope knowing this does not too greatly disturb you, for I do not wish to cause you unhappiness.*

Anabella, your presence would mean much to me as I engage in this duel, but I will not presume upon your goodwill by asking you a second time. It will take place in Terni, 15 March. I ask only that you pray for me, that I do not dishonor your family or myself.

If I am victorious—and I believe I will be—I shall come to you without any shame. I pray that my win will be sufficient to convince your brother to renew our betrothal. There is nothing I desire more.

With all my love,
Albret

Anabella carefully folded the letters and placed them in a box on her dressing table that held her precious items. Thrilled as she was to hear his warm words of love and devotion, she now faced a true dilemma. Two men desired her presence at the same duel. Each wanted her to witness his triumph over the other, thus establishing his honor. One man she had come to despise for his lies and trickery. The other she loved in spite of his foolishness.

What would be the influence of her presence on either? On both? If she went with Bianca to Terni, she most certainly would have to be a witness. And Albret's mother had even recommended she support her man. Marco would not prevent her and might very well be a witness himself. If she stayed in Florence, Albret said he would come to her; thus he didn't *expect* her to be present. That certainly would be the easier course.

&

"Albret, come in. The rapier we ordered from Toledo arrived today!" Malherbe exclaimed when he opened his door for Albret's final lesson. "I was just admiring it."

"Wonderful! I feared I might have to borrow one of yours, for mine certainly is not acceptable for dueling," said Albret. He followed the master into the fencing studio lit by candles that reflected in the mirrors. Malherbe went directly to the small table in the corner where the finished sword lay in all its shimmering glory.

"I know the craftsman myself. He is renowned throughout Spain and Italy. This smith turns out only a couple of such masterpieces a year, using precise and secret formulas to forge together the soft and hard steel with a high degree of heat; then he cools it with oil to achieve the correct tempering. As an item of masculine jewelry, it is unsurpassed in its splendor. But as a weapon, an opponent's very sight of it can bring about his defeat," said Malherbe, smiling broadly.

Albret picked up the sword in awe and ran his fingers along the sides of the smooth steel. The hardwood grip fit comfortably in his hand, and the elaborately carved silver guard equally fit his pride. Long and slender, the double edge almost seemed alive in his hand. "Then I will put my trust in it for a win tomorrow," he said with determination. "I think I am ready. Do you agree, Malherbe?"

"Indeed, I do. You've made amazing progress since you've put your heart into it. I see nothing to prevent a decided victory."

Albret placed himself in the initial stance for dueling, then sliced the air in mock engagement. "I love the feel of it—light yet strong." After several minutes of solo practice, he gently laid the rapier beside its scabbard on the table. "Let me fence today without protective paraphernalia—so I may sense the reality I will face tomorrow."

"As you wish," said Malherbe, "but even with buttoned tips on our foils, I could deal you a severe wound that would put you at a disadvantage against the conte."

"Vulnerable exposure today will set the tone for tomorrow," Albret pointed out.

"Very well. I admire your courage."

The two men took up their foils, crossed them, and launched into the maneuvers Albret had practiced. He felt in good form and warded off with skill all but the last attack by the master, after which the older man fell winded into his chair. Albret helped himself to a fresh towel and handed one to his partner. He had escaped with no more than a bruised rib from Malherbe's overzealous thrust.

"Had you actually been Frederico, as I imagined you to be, I would not have survived such a blow," Albret pointed out as they both wiped sweat from their faces.

"True. Though you have agreed only to first blood drawn, that blood could flow from a mortal wound," said the master. A servant woman brought in a pitcher of water and poured tankards for each of the men.

"Thank you. That will be all." When she had gone, Malherbe sipped his water thoughtfully, then leaned with his elbow on the table toward Albret. "You have learned well that fervor is as important as technique. But do not confuse freedom of movement with lack of control. You cannot afford even one mistake, one moment of distraction. Focus on the prize!"

And that prize is Anabella. Albret picked up his new rapier and carefully placed it in the scabbard. "Thank you, Malherbe. You are a friend as well as a teacher."

"I have invited a doctor I know to accompany us. I trust you do not object?" said Malherbe.

"Not at all. And I have asked my friend Massetti, who also works for the marchese, as a witness."

"What, no lady?"

Albret smiled as he recalled Anabella's horror when he had first mentioned the duel. "There is a lady who lives in Florence, but she does not wish to witness my being sliced to pieces before her very eyes."

"I see," said Malherbe with a chuckle. "Then the doctor and I will meet you on horseback outside the castle gates in about six hours, well before sunup. With tonight's full moon, we should have no trouble finding the spot on the knoll, I presume."

"No trouble at all."

"Sleep well, my friend." The two men shook hands. Albret mounted his steed and rode off into the night, soon to face his destiny.

&

Late in the afternoon of 14 March, a hired coach drew up to the Biliverti castle in Terni. Inside, fatigued from the long trip of several days in cramped quarters, Anabella held sleeping Pietro. She hoped Albret would see them from a window and rush out to greet her. But only a groomsman opened the gates for them.

The driver and a guardsman, who had traveled in front beside him, jumped down to assist the ladies from the carriage. Bianca descended first and received Pietro from Anabella's arms. The Soderini family had released Luisa and Giorgio to accompany them on the trip. It pleased Anabella to have Luisa with her again as her personal attendant. And Giorgio came as an extra bodyguard for the women on the journey.

Signora Sylvia Maseo stepped down last, and they all followed Anabella to the entrance, while the groom took care of the horses and coach.

Anabella, eager to see Albret and her brother, pulled the bell chain that hung above the doorway. Within a few moments, a house servant arrived to unlatch the doors. "Welcome home, Marchesa and signorina," said the woman. "Do come in. The marchese is in his study. I will announce your arrival."

"Give us a few minutes to refresh ourselves," said Bianca. "Then we will meet him in the salon."

Anabella rushed upstairs to her former room, which Marco had preserved just as she had left it more than two years ago. The musty smell did not dampen her joy of being back in the castle of her childhood. She unhooked the shutters, opened them wide, and breathed in the fresh air.

A servant boy knocked on the frame of the open door. "Signorina, I have brought up your baggage."

"Thank you. You may set it inside." When he had gone, she closed the door, opened a bag, and removed the dress she would wear to witness the duel. She shook it out and laid it across the back of a chair. On the top shelf of her armoire lay three hats. She took out each one, considered its fine points, chose the one with two pheasant feathers, and set it on the table. Since she would see Albret at dinner—if not before—she took special care in refreshing herself, arranging and tying back her hair.

She descended the staircase, her heart pounding in anticipation of encountering the man she loved—the man she had chosen to support in spite of her dislike for dueling.

In the salon, Marco and Bianca shared a double chair and a fond embrace. When Anabella entered, Marco rose to give her a brotherly hug. "It is so good to have you back in this house, 'Bella. I miss your laughter and conversation."

"I love being here—so many memories," she said, her face revealing the happiness she felt. "Everything is so different, the furnishings, the paintings... You have decorated beautifully, Bianca."

"Thank you, Anabella. I value your taste."

Marco returned to sit beside his wife, and Anabella took a chair near them. Luisa brought a tray with teakettle and cups, set it on a table, bowed, and left.

"I was just telling Bianca that the duel is to take place at sunrise tomorrow morning on the knoll we share with the Bargerinos," said Marco, placing his arm around Bianca's shoulders. "I am resigned to it."

"And where is Albret?" asked Anabella, looking around in hopes she would see him at any moment.

"We had received no message that you were coming," said Marco. "But he will be most pleased that you are here."

"Do you really think so?"

"Albret has always been steadfast in his love," said Marco. Bianca poured the herbal tea and handed out the cups. He sipped his tea, then continued. "Since Albret did not know you would be here, he and Massetti have gone to the tavern to dine with some fellows they know there."

"Then he should be back—"

"*Then* he has his final fencing lesson and will not be home until late."

Anabella's face fell with disappointment. She took one sip of tea and set her cup back on the tray. "He will win, don't you think?"

"I have reason to think so. His heart is in it," said Marco. "Like all young men today, he thinks he's defending his honor—and I might add, impressing the woman he loves."

"But it would impress me more if he had declined," said Anabella, not wishing to be part of his foolish decision.

"Marco just told me before you came in," said Bianca, "that he invited a priest over last night and had a special service for Albret in the family chapel."

"We prayed for his safety, courage, and success. And most

of all, that God's will be done. Though none of us approve of Albret accepting the challenge, we all support him," said Marco. He then stood, for they had been summoned to dinner. He shook his head and added, "I only hope he is not fighting in his own strength."

eighteen

Anabella awoke at the first cockcrow and quickly readied herself for the day. After donning the light blue dress with lace collar, she found her leather riding boots in the armoire and pulled them on. She awakened Luisa, who slept in the antechamber, and asked her to put up her hair.

"May Giorgio and I accompany you to the duel, signorina?" asked Luisa shyly as she tied a blue ribbon around Anabella's braided bun.

"Of course. I may need you. I've never witnessed such a duel either. It may be exciting or frightening. We shall see," said Anabella, taking a deep breath. After dusting off her hat and preening the feathers, she handed it and her long black cloak to Luisa. "Let's go downstairs." She hastily picked up a lighted candle in its holder and hoped that Albret had not as yet left. Seeing her would certainly give him encouragement.

Marco, Bianca, Signora Maseo, and Giorgio all stood in near darkness at the foot of the stairs. "Good morning, 'Bella." said Marco. "Hurry to the kitchen. We left bread and fruit for you. The carriage awaits."

"Has Albret already gone?"

"I barely had time to wish him Godspeed as he rushed out the door. He said his fencing master, who serves as his second, and a doctor were waiting."

"A doctor?"

With her hand at Anabella's back, Bianca steered her toward the kitchen. "Don't be concerned. Having a doctor present is only part of the ritual. It doesn't mean. . .well, blood will surely be drawn."

"Could he be killed?" Anabella asked with alarm. "I prayed for his safety last night."

"We have all prayed that God will be with him."

In the kitchen, Anabella took a bite of bread, but her stomach turned, and she ate no more. "Does he know I am here?"

"No one has had an opportunity to tell him," said Bianca. "Let's go face whatever the day may bring."

‹›

Fog hung in eerie layers as Albret and Massetti rode side by side, followed by Pierre de Malherbe and the doctor. Only the pounding of their horses' hooves broke the quiet. As they ascended the knoll, the mists gave way to predawn light. Their horses slowed, and Albret could hear a few awakening birds. Dead branches inhibited their progress as they passed through a strip of forest.

Suddenly the terrain opened up to a clearing at the top of the hill. They brought their horses to a halt. Albret looked up and saw the outline of Conte Frederico Bargerino and his entourage across the open space, still as statues, as though they had sat there astride their horses all night. In truth, Albret surmised they had arrived only minutes before.

"Wait here," said Malherbe dismounting. "I will approach Vasco." His counterpart, Frederico's second, likewise dismounted. The two crossed the field, shook hands, and conversed in low tones. After a few minutes, they motioned for the duelists to dismount and come forward.

Albret removed his feathered hat and cape and handed them to Massetti. Wearing a loose-fitting white shirt open at the throat and an unfastened vest for freer movement, he strode across the cool grass, damp with dew. His new rapier hung at his side. The conte, though only five years his senior, appeared much older with his beard and mustache and finely cut doublet. Both men unsheathed their swords and handed them to the seconds for inspection. Vasco searched Albret for a hidden dagger or potions of poison, while Malherbe did the same with the conte.

The principals made no acknowledgment of each other and returned to their supporters. The seconds marked the corners of the field of battle with piles of large stones. Through the bare tree branches, Albret detected a glow of red in the eastern sky. Hearing the sound of horses' hooves crashing through the underbrush, he turned and saw three of his friends from the tavern approaching. Their presence pleased him, but there was no sign of the marchese, who had hinted he might come as a reluctant witness.

His friends dismounted and chatted amiably with him. Then he heard voices, some of them feminine. Soon he could discern the marchese and a servant boy he didn't immediately recognize, holding aside the brambles to allow a group of ladies to pass without snagging their dresses.

Not until they emerged into the clearing did Albret recognize Bianca and his mother—and in the blue dress and black cloak, Anabella. Adjusting her hat, which had gone askew, she smiled broadly. Could this be a dream come to life? A rush of excitement swept over him. He took a step toward her, his arms outstretched. "You're here for me!" he whispered.

The voice of Guillermo Vasco broke into his joy. "Will the principals please step forward." Albret could only smile back at her before turning to the field of honor, where he took his place in the center next to Malherbe. He noticed a larger group of people assembling on the conte's side and beginning to merge with his witnesses. Shafts of light from the rising sun shot between the trees and striped the grassy field.

Vasco continued, "The combatants, Conte Frederico Bargerino and Signore Albret Maseo, have agreed to follow the *Code Duello*, and Pierre de Malherbe and myself are present to see that they do so. Conte Frederico has made this challenge to avenge an insult, in which *Signore* Maseo, without resorting to reason, labeled him a coward."

"And *Signore* Maseo has accepted the challenge in order to defend his honor, for indeed he spoke only what is well recognized as the truth," said Malherbe with a slight bow, his gray wisps of hair in wild disarray.

"The victory goes to the one who first draws blood or disarms his opponent. The duelists are then honor-bound to let the matter rest. No feud of family is to emerge after this contest," announced Vasco.

Albret watched the marchese make his way to the Bargerino side and shake hands with Signore and Signora Bargerino, Frederico's Terni relatives. Albret knew how important it was to the marchese to keep peace between the two families. The witnesses lined up at the edge of the forest, the pheasant-feathered hat and blue dress of Anabella plainly visible in the middle.

"In line!" shouted Vasco.

The two men saluted the audience with their swords, followed by deep bows. They took their places facing each other, again raised their swords in salute, and assumed the classic combat stance: the right toe pointing toward the opponent with the heel at the ankle of the left foot forming a ninety-degree angle. With knees slightly bent, left arm raised, they crossed swords.

"En garde!" shouted Malherbe.

Swords clashed with impeccable precision and echoed across the countryside. Albret realized the conte's skill matched his own. They engaged, attacked, parried. One, two, feint, withdraw, thrust. His confidence grew with the thrill of new steel and his own prowess. With agile footwork and quick timing, Albret felt himself gaining in the fray.

The audience remained silent except for an occasional collective gasp at a sudden thrust and rapid parry. Albret's anger rose toward the man responsible for so much sorrow, death, and destruction of commoners like himself. Out of the corner of his eye, Albret caught a glimpse of the blue dress, but he held his concentration.

Albret forced the conte to retreat several paces, spurred by his rising emotion. Their eyes met, and Albret could read as much fervent fire in his opponent as he himself felt. Between grunts, as steel clashed, Frederico growled through clenched teeth, "Anabella. . .is here. . .to applaud *me.*"

"Not true!" Albret shot back.

" 'Tis. I invited her. . . So your marchese. . .refused my proposal. She loves me!"

"Never!"

The conte made a vigorous attack, which Albret met too quickly, throwing off his timing.

"We plan. . .to elope!" The conte's sword swung high in the air and aimed toward Albret's neck.

Albret met steel with steel, catching his foe's rapier with the hilt of his own—but only slowing the blade that sliced into his right shoulder, close to his bare neck. Albret's fine-tempered rapier from Toledo tumbled to the ground. He slumped, clutching the wound that gushed blood between his fingers.

ðð

Anabella ran to Albret's side, overwhelmed and dismayed by the sudden turn of fortune. The doctor arrived ahead of her and stanched the wound with a padding of linen. He then ripped off Albret's vest and the right side of his shirt, leaving his chest bare. Hurriedly, he began wrapping strips of cloth over the gash, under his arm and around his body.

The smell of Albret's blood and sweat filled her nostrils. Pounding in her ears, she heard Frederico's voice shouting, "I am avenged! The honor is mine, and the liar dishonored." He stood behind Albret, blood sliding down his raised sword.

Albret sat, his eyes closed, supporting his head with his left hand, utterly defeated. Anabella reached her quivering hand out to him and whispered, "Albret."

He opened his eyes and stared at her as if she were a stranger. "Away from me, traitorous woman!" He waved his arm to shoo her off. "Did you come here to mock me?"

"No, no. You asked me," she murmured in shock at the rebuff.

A hand like a steel trap clenched her upper arm and pulled her up. "Let's go, my love," said a low but gruff voice.

All Albret's family and supporters crowded around him and thus failed to see Frederico pull the struggling Anabella with him across the field. She soon found herself engulfed by the conte's well-wishers, who were shouting his praises and drowning out her screams.

Over her shoulder, she saw Albret climb onto his horse with the help of Massetti and his fencing master. Marco stood with his arm around the distraught Bianca. All had their backs turned to Anabella, totally unaware of her plight. Except Giorgio. He spotted her just as Albret's friends, who had come on horseback, closed in around him and escorted him through the woods.

The Bargerino crowd brought out bottles of wine and passed them around, laughing uproariously and talking loudly. Only the older Bargerino couple, who had known Anabella since childhood, stood aside, looking somber and puzzled.

"Now we celebrate, my love," Frederico snarled, still gripping her arm.

Frightened and reeling from Albret's defeat and his words to her, she screamed "No!" over and over, but the group merely jeered.

Suddenly she saw the solemn face of Giorgio among the merrymakers. *"Per favore, signore,"* he said, looking directly at Frederico. "Please, release Signorina Anabella."

The rowdy crowd grew silent and stared at the slender youth. Frederico guffawed loudly and pushed Anabella away. "Go. You're no good to me without your dowry. I just wanted to further humiliate my foe. You're not worth fighting another duel over."

Weakened from the ordeal, she leaned on Giorgio for support as they headed back toward the family, who had just realized her absence. "You're a good man, Giorgio," she whispered. "A real hero."

At that moment, Marco ran up. "What happened to you? I'll carry you through the woods to the carriage. 'Bella, you are white as a ghost." His anxious face reassured her.

She smiled wanly at him. "I'm all right. It was just a mock kidnapping."

The others grouped around, dismayed and ashamed that something could have happened to her. "We saw you reach out to Albret ahead of any of us," said Bianca with remorse in her voice. "I noticed he spoke to you, but then you disappeared. We were all so worried about Albret."

Even amid her distress, Anabella noticed Luisa put her arm around Giorgio and heard him whisper, "Signorina says I am a hero."

"Let's go home," said Anabella. Albret's mother took one hand and Marco the other. Together they picked their way back through the brambles to the waiting carriage.

❧

Riding back in the carriage between Marco and Bianca, Anabella felt the love of those surrounding her. No words were needed. Across from her sat Signora Maseo, who endured her son's defeat with as much grief as she. Giorgio sat tall and straight as a hero should. How grateful she was for his bravery in rescuing her! And beside him sat loyal Luisa, her cheeks flushed by Giorgio's nearness.

Yet her heart ached not only over Albret's defeat, which reflected on all of them, and not only from worry over his wound, which might still prove fatal. She alone had heard his words of cold rejection. Those words would be difficult to repeat to anyone. Of all the confusing and startling events, this grieved her the most intensely.

She frowned at the irony of being harshly sent away by two men only minutes apart. And further, by the two men who had recently declared their love for her and invited her to witness their duel. The trauma of being snatched away by Frederico with its accompanying fear vied for her emotional energy.

She leaned back and closed her eyes. The rhythm of the carriage swaying over the rough ground soothed her. Frederico was not important, she decided. Only Albret mattered. His life immensely mattered. Their love mattered. Surely he had misunderstood something she had said or done. *I will go to him when we get back. When he is able, we will talk as we used to do in the little alcove by the kitchen, openly from the heart.*

nineteen

Albret lay on a cot in Malherbe's front room. The doctor knelt at his side, sponging the wound with an herbal solution. Malherbe's servant woman held the pan that the doctor repeatedly dipped his cloth into. Albret paid him little mind. He couldn't go back to the Biliverti castle, not since the marchese had lied about Anabella's letter—and withheld the man's name who had sought to betroth her. *The* marchese *must have told me her words of love so I would not be upset before the duel. Or because he still needs me as overseer until he can replace me.*

So Anabella had fallen for his enemy: Frederico Bargerino! It all seemed to make sense now. If Anabella had become so enamored with the conte that they wished to marry, how could she have changed her mind so suddenly? His anger rose again at the thought of carrying that letter to her brother—a letter that, no doubt, contained the expression of her love for Frederico, not himself. The marchese had been upset at Anabella for wanting to marry the leader of the unjust war against the peasants. Thus he had concluded he should find a different husband for her. He and Anabella must have conspired to keep the identity of her pursuer secret from him.

"Hold still, Albret. We're about finished here," said the doctor. "I know this is painful."

Not as painful as the hurt inside!

Albret sat up so the doctor could bind his arm to his chest.

"There, that should do it," said the doctor, seemingly satisfied with his work. "Keep that arm immobile for a while so as not to pull the cut apart. You're a lucky man. If he had struck the main neck artery, you could have bled to death."

Albret chose not to respond. He struggled to insert his left arm into a clean shirt that Malherbe had placed on the cot. The servant tried to help, but Albret shrugged her away. He pulled the shirt over his right shoulder and bound arm, then managed to button it at the bottom. He felt some dizziness as he rose and walked over to the table where Malherbe was sitting.

"I'll be back tomorrow to check on our patient," said the doctor and let himself out.

"It's humiliating even to be alive," mumbled Albret, pulling a wooden chair out and seating himself.

"No, no," said Malherbe. "Very disappointing, yes. But a defeat can only be cured by a successful win. Tell me, what happened? Did Frederico insult you?"

The servant brought Albret a cup of willow bark tea. "This will ease your pain, signore," she said, setting it down before him.

"Thank you," said Malherbe. "You may go home now." The woman gathered up a small bundle of laundry, including Albret's bloody shirt, bowed, and exited.

Albret sipped the tea. Clear images of those fateful minutes sprang to life in his memory. He relived them as he related everything to Malherbe: the missed timing, the technical errors, and Frederico's words about Anabella. "He had just said they intended to elope when he made that lunge, and I fell. Anabella came running up. No sooner had I dismissed her for betraying me, than I saw Frederico reach for her. She disappeared with him through the crowd—and I never saw her again."

"His taunt was calculated to provoke you and throw you off," said Malherbe. "Perhaps he lied about intending to marry Anabella." The old man got up and went to the fire where there hung a pot of potato soup that his servant had prepared. He dipped up two bowls and set them on the table along with a half loaf of bread, then filled two tankards.

"I don't think he lied," said Albret, shaking his head. "Someone recently asked the marchese for an impalmare agreement with her. I didn't realize then that it was none other than my foe."

"Hmm," contemplated Malherbe as he spooned soup into his mouth. "Do you remember I told you Frederico had lost much of his wealth and was forced to sell the land he had wanted to rid of peasants?"

"Yes, and you said something about his wanting to marry a lady for her large dowry," said Albret. He laid down his spoon and wiped his chin with a napkin.

"And lands."

"That would be Anabella," said Albret, suddenly enlightened. "That scoundrel!"

"There's certainly reason for another duel somewhere in all this!" shouted Malherbe, raising his spoon for emphasis.

Anabella's energy returned as the carriage approached the castle. At the gate, she quickly descended without help from Luisa or anyone else. Inside, she ran first to Albret's room by the kitchen and knocked on the door. "Albret? Albret?" When no answer came, she ran up the stairs, still calling his name.

By the time the others had come in, she was descending the staircase. "He doesn't seem to be here. The servants haven't seen him." Her face felt drawn with anxiety. "Where would he have gone?"

"Perhaps they were forced to ride slowly because of his injury," reasoned Marco.

What if he lies dying somewhere? Or did he not come here because of me?

"We would have passed them on the way," suggested Bianca. "He wouldn't be well enough to go to the tavern, would he?"

"I don't know, but I'm puzzled about something," said Marco. "Let's all go sit at the table—it's about time for lunch to be served—and we can discuss the situation. You come, too, Sylvia."

They all followed Marco and took places around the table.

"Of course Albret was in a great deal of pain and no doubt dejected because of his loss, but how did he react to each of you?" asked Marco.

"He thanked me when I laid his cape across his shoulders," said Bianca.

"He lovingly squeezed my hand," said Signora Maseo. "He told me not to worry, that it wasn't too serious. I hardly believed him with all that loss of blood."

"And 'Bella, you had already. . .well, you weren't there when he left," said Marco. "How are you feeling?"

"I'm just so worried about Albret." *I cannot tell them the awful things he said to me.* "You said something puzzled you."

"Yes. I don't know what to make of it. Albret knows I think highly of him, though I tried to persuade him to reject this challenge. We've had other disagreements, too, but he has always treated me with the utmost respect. However, when I took his arm to assist him in mounting his horse, he jerked it away and stared at me in such an alarming manner I could not interpret it. He then allowed Massetti and his fencing master to attend him. Perhaps that isn't significant."

"It's certainly strange. Massetti has already gone home to his family, or we could ask him about Albret's whereabouts," said Bianca.

The servants brought out mutton stew, bread, pasta, fruit, and cheese. Marco said a short blessing, everyone crossed themselves, and then they began to eat in silence. Anabella's worry grew.

Albret's mother was the first to speak. "I think he could be recovering at the fencing master's house."

"Then I will go to him," said Anabella, putting down her spoon and standing up.

"I think it best that I take Sylvia in the carriage," said Marco. "I'll wait outside while she goes in. He certainly will not reject his mother. If he is not there, at least the fencing master should know where we can find him."

"As you wish, Marco," said Anabella as she sat down.

Signora Maseo rose and put her arm around Anabella's shoulders. "He's only ashamed of his loss, signorina. We'll find him," she said gently. "I know how much he loves you."

&

In spite of the delicious taste of revenge, Albret had no desire to think about another duel. He claimed fatigue, returned to his cot, and fell fast asleep. A loud knock at the door awakened him. He sat up to answer it, thinking he was in his own bed. Pain shot across his shoulder and down his arm. He watched as Malherbe opened the door to a fencing student and the two headed off to the studio closing the door after them.

No sooner had he closed his eyes again and pulled a blanket under his chin than another tapping disturbed him. He lay still several minutes, not wanting to get up. Certainly Malherbe would not hear this visitor. The tapping came again. And then a third time. Carefully he dragged himself up to a sitting position. He looked down at his boots on the floor and knew he could not pull them on with one hand. Were he not here, no one would answer the door. Why not ignore it? The knock came again, with more urgency. All right, he would be a gentleman.

He walked over, lifted the latch, and opened the door a crack. "Mother! What are you doing here?"

"May I come in?"

"Of course." He pulled out a chair for her at the table and then sat down himself.

"Tell me how you are." She touched his cheek with the back of her hand as he remembered her doing when illness would strike him as a child.

"I'm all right, Mother. The villain missed the artery. The doctor has given me good care and will check on me again tomorrow. How did you know where I was?"

"A mother knows. But we are all concerned. You need not be ashamed around those who love you. There is no need to hide out like this." She frowned and patted his knee.

"Don't pity me, Mother. I will overcome this—somehow." Albret took her hand. It felt rough from years of work. "I cannot go back to the Bilivertis. I want you to come with me to Padua—where I can study law. I have money. You will have a girl to serve you for a change."

"Albret, I don't know what you are talking about. How could you have enough to support both of us? And I couldn't leave Bianca. She's like a daughter that I've raised since her early childhood. The Bilivertis treat us very well, almost like family members."

"Mother, the Bilivertis have betrayed me." He searched her questioning eyes. "Didn't you see Anabella?"

"What? You think Anabella betrayed you? The girl is worried sick about you. Where did you get such notions? She wanted to come here herself, but the marchese said only I should talk to you."

"The marchese. How dare—"

"After the trauma of her kidnapping by that horrible Bargerino, Anabella has shown great strength." His mother folded her hands and closed her eyes as if reliving the event.

"What do you mean by 'kidnapping,' Mother?" Apparently the vivid scenes in his head did not match his mother's memory of the same.

"None of us saw that monster drag her off, either, but she told us all about it. I thought you, at least, would have had your eyes on Anabella and seen what happened. She was right in front of you. Of course, we were all concerned for you and didn't take notice. What do you mean 'betrayed'?"

"I thought she went willingly," Albret mumbled, trying to understand.

"Hardly. Even after that, all she's been concerned about is you, Albret. She came all the way from Florence to witness your duel—because you asked her. Because she loves you. She told me that herself."

His mother continued to tell the story of Giorgio's bravery and Frederico's claim to have no need for her without her dowry. "I must go now. The marchese is waiting in the carriage. Won't you come home with us?" Her eyes pleaded. But his mind swirled with the new reality he wished to believe.

"Not now, Mother, but soon. I have a lot of thinking to do." He turned the next words over in his mind, wanting to be certain. Finally, he said, "Tell Anabella not to worry. I will come to her."

☙

Four days had passed since Signora Maseo had related her conversation with Albret. Anabella sat on a window seat upstairs at the front of the castle. With shutters open wide, she leaned out and surveyed the rounded hills of vineyards bathed in morning sunlight. The world was coming to life with the onset of spring: patches of green grass, wild plum trees in bloom, and a pair of wrens building their nest on a nearby limb. *When will he come to me?* She looked toward the private road that led up the hill to the castle.

In the distance, a lone horseman came into view, emerging from behind a cliff off the main road. She watched the horse trotting resolutely and tried to determine the identity of the rider. Albret, being wounded, surely would be brought home in a carriage. As he drew closer, she squinted her eyes. Could it be? When he arrived at the gate, all doubt vanished.

"Albret!" she shouted and waved. He looked up, lifted his good arm toward her, and then dismounted. She ran rapidly down the stairs and arrived at the front doors just as he pulled the bell rope. Before a servant could arrive, she lifted the latch and flung open the doors. There stood Albret, handsome as ever, with his arm in a sling.

"Anabella, my love, my joy, my future!" He swept his left arm around her, nearly whisking her off her feet, and planted a kiss firmly on her lips. "I love you, Anabella. Will you marry me?"

"I answered that question once before," she said with a

laugh. "That answer still holds—if Marco will again consent."

Albret held her close, kissed her forehead, her eyes, again her mouth. "Let me hear you say it again."

"I love you, Albret." She encircled her arms about him, gently over the injured side. "Yes. I will marry you."

twenty

Albret and Anabella found their way to the simple alcove by the kitchen. Marco, Bianca, and Albret's mother had all gone into Terni to make some purchases in anticipation of spring. A nursemaid watched over the sleeping Pietro upstairs. Thus, except for the servants, the two were alone in the castle.

Albret wore his dueling shirt, obviously laundered, and vest, his arm supported by a scarf tied about his neck.

"You appear in marvelous health, Albret. How are you?"

"The cut is healing quickly. No infection this time, thanks to the doctor's quick care."

They sat side by side on the bench beneath the small window. Albret took her hand in his. "We have so much to talk about. I have been wrong in so many ways. Anabella, I am sorry for rejecting you after my defeat. Frederico had just told me you loved him and the two of you were going to elope because your brother would not consent to your marriage. Mother has explained to me the truth."

"Albret, I had fallen for his flattery out of my loneliness."

"I know. I should not have released you from our betrothal."

"I never really considered marrying him. He only wanted my dowry." She smoothed out the skirt of her brown housedress trimmed in ivory lace and pulled a handkerchief from her sleeve. "Please forgive me for my foolishness."

"Of course. But also forgive me." He put his good arm about her shoulders and pulled her close. "I confess I have made many errors in judgment, Anabella."

"Losing the duel makes no difference in my esteem for you, Albret," she said, looking into his eyes. "You were an honorable man before, and you are honorable now."

"It's true. Honor does not depend on winning a duel or in gaining wealth and position. Where I have been dishonorable is in putting my faith in a sword and in my own skill. After all, 'pride goeth before destruction.' That's what really brought about my fall—failing to place my trust in the Lord God."

"We have a forgiving God," she said and dabbed the corners of her eyes, overcome with the emotion of the moment.

"I have asked His forgiveness. Since Mother's visit at Malherbe's, I have spent the time in deep contemplation and prayer, trying to find my true values."

"And what did you find, Albret?"

"I did not like what I discovered about myself. This whole idea of trying, in my own power, to become worthy of you may have been a striving for my own glory. I forgot to be humble. But what I now know is that God and his teachings must always be foremost. Then love. You will be my partner in life, so I will always love you first, then work to help my fellow man."

"That's what you did in fighting for the peasants' cause."

"Yes, that was just. But I need not have set you aside to do so."

"Did I not tell you as much?" she said with a teasing smile.

"You were right about many things," he said, grinning back at her. "Anabella, do you remember a little plaque that you embroidered in red for your brother several years ago? It hangs in his study."

"Something about wisdom and humility. . .perhaps honor?"

"That's the one. 'The fear of the Lord is the instruction of wisdom; and before honour is humility.' The marchese showed it to me once, trying to convince me to reject the challenge to duel. My father had refused such a challenge and was murdered anyway. At first, my acceptance of the duel was to establish my honor and to somehow avenge his death. But as I trained with the fencing master, I became prideful."

"I didn't know about your father."

"I'll tell you more sometime," he said with a smile and stood up. "It's a lovely spring day, and I need exercise. Let us go for a walk and enjoy God's blessings."

They slipped out the back door by the kitchen. Anabella breathed in the fresh air. "I wonder if the daffodils are blooming by the well. They are among the first flowers of spring, and I love to gather them," she said.

As they walked through the formal garden, they passed two workers clearing out the dead vines of winter and preparing for new plants. Albret struggled with the rusted iron latch of the side gate. It creaked as he swung it open. "I'll have to fix that," he mumbled to himself. They followed a path around the sidewall of the castle to the ancient well built of stones. Indeed, the yellow trumpet flowers were bursting into bloom in little clusters all around. The smell of fresh earth warmed by the sun hung in the air.

"As a child, I used to come out here to read," said Anabella, sitting on the edge of the well. She reached down, plucked a flower, and sniffed its fragrance.

"I used to see you here as I set off to my chores," said Albret, placing his hand on her knee. Anabella put her hand over his. "Anabella, you have agreed to marry me without considering how we will live."

"I've considered," she said. "I do love beautiful things, but what I really enjoy about decorating a home is seeing how colors and shapes fit together in an artistic manner. I can do that even in a humble cottage. Things have never been as important to me as people. I adore the orphan children we have nourished—watching them learn and grow. And I love you, Albret. I want to be wherever you are."

She kissed him softly on the lips. "You never asked me if I wanted to rescind the betrothal. You just assumed I would want more of this world's goods than you could give me. I think that is what this misunderstanding was all about."

"Again, I was wrong to assume anything about you. I thought I needed to do something more to earn your love— love which you had already given me. Perhaps I really wanted to be proud of myself." He got up and—awkwardly with only one hand—picked more than a dozen daffodils and handed them to her.

"Thank you." She smiled up at him.

"Anabella, do you believe your brother will forgive me?"

"He will forgive us both," she said, lowering her eyelashes and smiling sweetly. "Marco is gruff sometimes, but he always wants what is best for his little sister."

"When you look at him like that, I'm sure he indulges your every whim." He chuckled and added, "And as your husband— if he permits our marriage—I'll probably do the same."

He took his seat beside her again. "I've thought a great deal about our future, Anabella. After the marchese agrees, our betrothal ceremony can be held wherever and whenever you choose. I could work another year for him and save some money. Then we could marry."

"One year is good, but don't forget about my dowry." She buried her nose in the bouquet and breathed in deeply. "And don't be offended, but I would love to live here on the land of my ancestors."

"Eventually, perhaps." He frowned. "After you are my wife, I would like to move to Padua for a few years and study law at the university. What do you think?"

"I think that is an exciting idea," she said with sincere enthusiasm. "You never told me you were interested in law."

"I would like to defend the scientists like Bruno and Clavius and Galileo that your brother is always talking about. Or any worthy cause that needs defending. When I met with the emissary in Pisa, he said King Philip would like to call on me from time to time whenever he needs a good negotiator."

"What an honor! He must have been very impressed by your plea," she said with admiration.

"And the king sent me a sum of money as an award, taken from a fine he imposed on my foe, Conte Bargerino."

"That is certainly justice!" she exclaimed, trying to conceal a laugh. "But why didn't you tell me before?"

"I think you had an urgent need to get back to a dress you were making," he said and kissed away her words of protest.

"All right, that was foolish on my part," she finally said after struggling free. She laughed and returned to the subject of their future. "Perhaps in Padua I could earn some money for us as a master designer."

"If you so wish to use your talents. But Anabella, the award was quite a large sum of money. With it and your dowry, we could rent a small townhouse, perhaps even employ one servant. And I could work as a bookkeeper for a small business after my classes. I think your brother would write me a letter of commendation based on my keeping of his ledgers."

"And do you suppose your mother could come live with us in Padua?" Anabella suggested. "I have come to admire her so much and enjoy her company."

"I think we might convince her of that," he said.

❧

Back in the castle, Anabella put the daffodils in a pottery jar and brought them into the salon. At that moment, the family returned from their shopping in Terni. Signora Maseo and Luisa carried bundles to the kitchen, and Giorgio hauled bags of grain to an underground storage area. Marco and Bianca came directly into the salon and discovered Albret standing in the middle of the room and Anabella setting the vase of flowers on the mantle.

Bianca ran to Albret, kissed him on the cheek, and said, "You look well, Albret. I'm so glad you have come home."

Marco approached, shook his hand, and said, "I hope your dueling days are over, my friend."

"Indeed, they are," Albret said. And without further ado, he continued with what lay uppermost in his mind. "Marchese, you have expressed your intention of finding a suitable husband for your sister. I would like to offer you myself to fill that role. I ask again for the hand of Anabella, whom I love with all my heart." Anabella came and stood smiling beside him.

Marco revealed obvious pleasure in this announcement but said, "And can you assure me of your steadfastness, young man? Do you agree never to leave my sister bereft again, until death itself do you part?"

"I do so agree," said Albret with a broad grin. "And to the *impalmare*—if it is still in effect—I am able to add a bag of silver coins."

Marco's eyebrows shot upward. "The recorded agreement is, indeed, still in place."

"And the purse was awarded to me by King Philip himself," Albret said behind his hand to Marco.

Marco nodded, apparently content with the brief explanation. "Then it is settled at long last. Congratulations to the happy couple."

"I, too, am delighted for you both," added Bianca, hugging Anabella, then Albret.

"What is this I hear, signora?" asked Signora Maseo, coming in from the kitchen, followed by Luisa. Giorgio entered quietly from the back door and stood next to Luisa.

"Your son and Anabella are finally going to be betrothed." Bianca said, revealing her happiness.

"A very wise decision, Son," she said and kissed him on the cheek. "A most wise and honorable choice." She added a kiss to Anabella's cheek as well.

"While we are making announcements," said Bianca, "Giorgio and Luisa told us that—Giorgio, why don't you tell them?"

"If you wish, signora," said Giorgio, blushing and taking Luisa's hand. "Luisa and I wish to marry, also."

"But Signora Soderini told me I must find new employment," said Luisa, looking down, "so that will separate us. Since Signora Cecilia is married, her mother no longer has need of my services."

Everyone expressed happiness and encouragement to the

young servants, including Anabella who added, "I thought I noticed a bond between the two of you. I owe much to you, Giorgio, for rescuing me from that evil conte. When my mother hears about that, I'm sure she will agree to allow Luisa to return to us as my personal attendant. You will be close enough to see each other on Sundays until you are married. Then we will see what arrangements can be made."

The girl's face glowed with gratitude. She clasped her hands together and said, "Thank you, signorina. I would like very much to serve you."

❧

The following week flew by quickly. Albret returned to his duties as overseer, which included supervising the turning of soil, birthing of lambs, and checking the vineyards. By week's end, his wound had healed sufficiently to discontinue the sling.

Anabella spent her time helping Luisa and Mother Sylvia—as she now called her—make cheese and bread. And playing with little Pietro. Occasionally she sat with Bianca, crocheting a shawl for her mother and talking about her future as a student's wife in Padua.

"Are you eager to renew your work on the Jacob painting, Bianca?" Anabella said one afternoon as they sat on the window seat that overlooked the front gate. Both enjoyed this spot, flooded with daylight, for doing handwork.

"Yes, of course. I hate to leave anything unfinished. But I shall have to work quickly to complete it before we come back here in June for your betrothal ceremony. Mother Costanza may want to come even earlier to supervise the planning."

"She will be pleased, don't you think?"

"Your mother and Father Antonio both will be quite pleased—and relieved," said Bianca, pulling through a thread of embroidery. "You know, Anabella, the sculptor who is creating the statues for your ballroom has relatives in Padua. If you are really interested in gaining commissions as a master decorator, he could recommend you to clients he knows. He often spends several months of the year there."

"Do you really think that is possible—I mean for me, a mere girl?" Anabella said, laying aside the shawl she was working on.

"Of course. I won a competition for a church altarpiece when I was barely seventeen," said Bianca. "That started my career. Women are being recognized more and more."

"I'll be seventeen by the time we are married," she said. "Albret hopes to take on evening work, so I will certainly have time. We have asked Luisa and Giorgio to come with us, if Mother and Papa Antonio agree. Albret will try to find an apprenticeship for Giorgio in a trade, and Luisa can help me around the cottage. I won't mind at all living more simply."

"Anabella, Marco plans to talk to Albret before we leave tomorrow about granting you a portion of this seigniory as an inheritance. Marco has always been forward looking. He thinks it makes little sense for the eldest son to inherit everything and leave the siblings nothing—which today is the general rule. When Albret has finished his studies, you can come back here and have a villa built. Marco thinks Albret should invest that 'bag of silver' with my father, who is in the banking business in Rome."

Anabella thought of the miniature villa sitting on her dressing table in Florence, the signore waving to his signora in the upstairs window. "Before, Marco always referred to the land as a gift. I don't know if Albret could so easily reject my *inheritance*," said Anabella. "He is no longer so prideful. But either way, rich or poor, I shall be happy with him."

ka

The next morning, the hired coach had pulled up to the front gates, and Giorgio and the driver were loading the baggage. Anabella and Albret sought out the little alcove for a few minutes alone. She had brewed Albret some of Papa Antonio's coffee that she had brought especially for him—and forgotten until now. She set the tray on the little table and poured the two cups half full, then added steaming milk. As she handed

Albret his cup, she said, "I wish this were our wedding day instead of my going away from you."

"We've made our most important decision," said Albret, holding his cup in both hands and taking a sip. "It saddens me to see you leave, but at least we know we are committed to each other. I need the year to grow in my faith and prepare for my new responsibilities as your husband. Only the Lord God knows what lies ahead."

"Mother and Papa Antonio will bring me back for our betrothal ceremony in about two months." She sat her cup aside and took Albret's hand.

"I will write to you often and come visit in the fall after harvest," said Albret, looking intensely into her eyes.

"And perhaps at Christmastime," said Anabella, "we can go listen to the shepherds who come down from the hills to play their bagpipes."

"We can start our own presepio with a Santo Bambino."

"And our miniature villa."

Luisa suddenly appeared and said, "Pardon me, but the marchesa says to come as we are leaving now." She bowed and hurriedly left.

They both stood, still holding hands, and faced each other. From inside his doublet, Albret pulled a letter, sealed and addressed to Signore and Signora Turati. "Would you take this to your parents? I hold them in high esteem."

"This is several pages," she said, surprised, as she took the letter.

"I had a lot to confess and to thank them for. I want them to consider me worthy of marrying their daughter."

Albret then took Anabella in his arms, drew her close to his body, and placed his warm, moist lips fervently on hers. She closed her eyes and yielded to their mutual passion. The thrill of love and happiness flooded over her.

"You will never be far from me, Anabella, for I will hold you forever close within my heart."

"I love you, Albret," she whispered and returned his kiss with equal fervor.

He took her hand, and together they walked out to the waiting coach, ready to face whatever their future might hold.

A Letter To Our Readers

Dear Reader:

In order that we might better contribute to your reading enjoyment, we would appreciate your taking a few minutes to respond to the following questions. We welcome your comments and read each form and letter we receive. When completed, please return to the following:

Fiction Editor
Heartsong Presents
PO Box 719
Uhrichsville, Ohio 44683

1. Did you enjoy reading *Duel Love* by Barbara Youree?
   ❑ Very much! I would like to see more books by this author!
   ❑ Moderately. I would have enjoyed it more if

   _____

   _____

   _____

2. Are you a member of **Heartsong Presents**? ❑ Yes ❑ No
   If no, where did you purchase this book? _____

   _____

3. How would you rate, on a scale from 1 (poor) to 5 (superior), the cover design? _____

4. On a scale from 1 (poor) to 10 (superior), please rate the following elements.

   ____ Heroine   ____ Plot
   ____ Hero   ____ Inspirational theme
   ____ Setting   ____ Secondary characters

5. These characters were special because? _____
_____
_____

6. How has this book inspired your life? _____
_____
_____

7. What settings would you like to see covered in future
   Heartsong Presents books? _____
_____
_____

8. What are some inspirational themes you would like to see
   treated in future books? _____
_____
_____

9. Would you be interested in reading other **Heartsong
   Presents** titles? ❑ Yes ❑ No

10. Please check your age range:
   ❑ Under 18   ❑ 18–24
   ❑ 25–34   ❑ 35–45
   ❑ 46–55   ❑ Over 55

Name _____
Occupation _____
Address _____
City, State, Zip_____

Presents

Great Inspirational Romance at a Great Price!

Heartsong Presents books are inspirational romances in contemporary and historical settings, designed to give you an enjoyable, spirit-lifting reading experience. You can choose wonderfully written titles from some of today's best authors like Peggy Darty, Sally Laity, DiAnn Mills, Colleen L. Reece, Debra White Smith, and many others.

When ordering quantities less than twelve, above titles are $2.97 each.
Not all titles may be available at time of order.